FLACK

GUARDIAN SECURITY SHADOW WORLD

KRIS MICHAELS

CHAPTER 1

*T**wo weeks before the Siege**:*

FLACK WAITED SILENTLY as his target entered the garden. The sliver of a crescent moon provided little light, and the man in front of him didn't turn on the outdoor lamps. Instead, he thumbed a cigarette into his mouth and flicked the lighter, illuminating his face with an orange hue. A flip of the cap extinguished the flame as the man inhaled deeply and blew the smoke from his lungs, sending the scent of tobacco and a hint of the tinny smell of lighter fluid through the air. Flack remained still, covered from his target's view. He watched as the soon-to-be-dead man moved to the bench he sat on every night.

Flack's eyes shifted to the right, then the left. No guards, as usual. He waited until the monster sat down on the bench and only then, shielded by a hedgerow, moved soundlessly over the manicured lawn.

"Hello?"

Flack froze at the sound of his target's voice. *Had he been seen? No.* There was no way.

"What is it you need tonight, my friend?" His target laughed. "No, no, I have a good supply of just your type. What? Two? Of course. I'll have them sent. Yes, tonight." His target laughed again. "No, no payment. Just remember me when I need a favor in return." Flack moved to the edge of the hedgerow, waiting for the conversation to end. He could see Norman Rink, cigarette in one hand, phone in the other by his ear. "Goodnight, and enjoy."

The target placed his phone on the bench and leaned back, inhaling another lungful of toxic chemicals. Flack lifted his blow gun to his lips. The tiny stream of the red laser landed on the target's neck, and Flack fired the dart. It hit and held in Rink's neck. The man jolted forward. His phone clattered through the wooden slats of the bench, dropping with a muted thud to the grass below. Flack moved forward and carefully examined his surroundings. No sound from the house or the pool area. Reaching Rink, he pushed the man back up into a seated position. His mark's eyes bulged.

Flack took the target's phone and pocketed it. "You can't move. You can't speak. The poison in your system will stop your heart in less than two minutes."

Rink's mouth moved, but there was no sound other than the flap of flesh against flesh. "Are you asking why or who?" Flack said. He glanced at the man staring back at him. "You're evil, and we both know you are one hundred percent guilty. The evidence?" Flack sat down on the bench with the man. He looked up at the sky. "Three hundred and forty-seven people murdered on your command in Africa. Blood diamonds flooding the market through your conveyance. Thousands of innocent people are dying in those diamond mines. To put a cherry on top of it, you're in bed with the Bratva, selling the children of those you murdered into the sex market. The world might not be able to convict you, but the council has."

Flack listened as the man's breathing slowed.

Rink might not have heard Flack's words, but it didn't matter. Flack had compiled the detailed review of his completed case last week and submitted it through secure channels to Archangel.

Four days later, the secret multi-national council coded Rink. Flack had no doubt of the man's guilt. He'd researched every law the man had broken and provided irrefutable evidence of his guilt to the council. *That* was his specialty. It was what he did for Guardian that no one else did. He was called in to research the men and women the council believed were guilty of abominations against the world. Still, the evidence they acquired had to be checked to warrant it wasn't tainted, biased, or weak. He put the multi-agency intel reports and the law together. His role was investigator, litigator, and, in some cases, executioner. The council was the judge and jury. Each case took many months of exhaustive effort to research and prepare. Evidence, human intelligence, and electronic surveillance either substantiated the charges against his targets or exonerated them. Flack spent countless months ensuring the target's guilt or innocence was painstakingly annotated and triple-checked. There was no room for error when dealing with a death sentence. Flack didn't make mistakes. He would not be rushed, and his cases, when completed, were infallible.

The man who'd stopped breathing beside him was a monster of the highest caliber. The stacks of information and evidence left no room for any doubt in Flack's or the council's mind. He knew if Rink had been arrested for his crimes, he would have used his money, connections, and favors to get out of the charges, or he would have fled to another country. He'd managed to escape prosecution for years. His reign of terror would have continued, but not anymore. Flack took out an alcohol swab and dabbed at the blood trickling down the side of the man's neck. Holding the swab over the entrance wound, he pulled out the dart and secured it in a metal vial from his pocket. He then opened a small container and smoothed some of the contents over the dart's puncture wound. After waiting thirty seconds, he wiped the area with another swab. The puncture wouldn't be detected now as the contents the container mimicked human skin and, even in the stages of decomposition, would hold its integrity. The autopsy would show a heart attack killed Rink. Flack hoped the man would roast in hell.

Flack checked that his equipment was stowed

KRIS MICHAELS

before he carefully and silently made his way out
of the compound using the same entry route to
exit. There would be no indication he had been
there. He was, after all, more than just an assassin.
He was a Shadow.

*Present Day. **Virginia.***

FLACK STOOD in the hall staring through the glass
at where his niece lay in a hospital crib. She was
beautiful and looked just like his sister and mother.
Her dark brown hair partly obscured her face, but
her cupid bow lips and perky little nose were so
familiar. The family resemblance was unmistak-
able, but the reality of his niece lying in that crib
seemed unreal. Emotionally he felt distant, sepa-
rated by more than just the glass between them.
"Excuse me, can I help you?"

Flack turned his attention to a woman in
scrubs and pointed to Brooke's crib. "She's my
niece. I was just informed she was brought here."

"Which one?"

"Brooke Shankle." He pointed again to the
crib.

"Oh, have you talked to Mrs. Pruitt? She's in the nurse's lounge. I can get her for you."

"Mrs. Pruitt?" He had no idea who that was.

"Brooke's case worker. Actually, Mrs. Pruitt has several young ones in the hospital right now. Unfortunately, she's a permanent fixture around here. Hold on for a minute. I'll get her for you."

Flack crossed his arms and looked at the cribs in the big room. Ten in all, some equipped with machines and tubes going to the little ones. Others, like Brooke's, were just metal cribs. Cartoon animals were painted on the walls as if the staff had tried to make it less of a hospital environment.

He heard the footsteps coming his way and glanced down the hall. A stout, portly woman, probably mid-fifties, trundled toward him. Her gray hair was cut shoulder length, and she smiled at him. "Mr. Masters?"

"Troy, please." Flack extended his hand. "Would you please tell me what happened? How did she end up here?"

"Well, a neighbor heard Brooke coughing excessively and crying for an extended period. She called the police, who went to the Shankles' house. This is the fifth time the police or social services have been called since she was placed. The grand-parents seemed to overestimate their ability to keep up with her."

Flack cracked his neck. "I'm a lawyer. Please speak plainly. What exactly are we talking about?"

Mrs. Pruitt drew a deep breath and shook her head. "Were they negligent? Yes. Were they trying to be?" She shook her head. "I can't prove that. But as they haven't started guardianship paperwork and since they want to give up the temporary custody they currently have, I don't know if we'll be pursuing criminal charges."

"What? Why not?" *That* was unacceptable.

"Do you see those cribs? With the exception of two—Brooke being one—these innocent babies are all here as a result of horrible abuse cases. The difference between abuse and neglect is as wide as the Grand Canyon. Brooke is one of the lucky ones. She has you."

"I'm not a prize, and I don't know if I can take her." He was single, had no clue how to raise a kid, let alone a little girl, and to top all that off, he was a fucking assassin. Plus, that little girl needed someone who would be there for her. He wasn't sure he could make that commitment.

"Come sit down and talk with me for a

minute." Mrs. Pruitt started down the hall, and damn him, Flack fell into step next to her. "What is your primary concern?" she asked as she stopped at an alcove with hard blue plastic seats.

Flack sat across from her and dropped his elbows to his knees. "Where do I start? I'm single. I have no idea how to raise a kid. I travel extensively, and I'm out of the country for months at a time."

Mrs. Pruitt chuckled. "I would be over the moon to place any of these babies with a single parent who would love and protect them. Let me ask you something. Do you have the financial ability to provide for Brooke?"

Flack frowned at the woman. "Money isn't a concern. My *ability* is." He'd received half of his parents' inheritance, and his work for Guardian provided more than he could ever spend. He'd never have to worry about money. Trisha had inherited the other half of their parents' fortune. From what he understood from talking with Trisha's lawyers after her death, it was held in trust for Brooke's benefit.

"Then have you considered hiring someone to live with you to provide care? Someone to help out when you're at work. A person who could care for the baby while you're on your trips."

"A nanny?" A vision of a prim and proper woman floating out of the sky holding an umbrella flashed into his head. He chuffed out a sad laugh. "Yeah, not sure that would work." Rubbing the back of his neck, he sighed. He'd have to make sure any permanent nanny was vetted by Guardian. There were so many things outside the norm regarding his taking custody.

"Well, there's a lot to think about, and taking on a child is a lifetime commitment." Mrs. Pruitt sighed. "I can place Brooke in a foster home for a short time. Most of the people I routinely use are already caring for infants, so it may be a day or so before I can place her."

Troy flopped back on his chair. "I've also heard horror stories about the foster care system." Damn it. There was no winning in the situation, especially for that little girl.

"The bad stories do get publicity, but there are wonderful people out there who have a lot of love to give." Mrs. Pruitt smiled. "I do need to place her, however. She's taking up a crib that's needed." She stood up.

"When?" Flack popped to his feet.

"Soon, I'm afraid. Brooke is past the worst part of the RSV. The cough is getting better, and her oxygen level is good. She doesn't need around-the-clock care. At this point, what she needs is love and positive attention."

Flack dropped his head back and looked at the ceiling. He couldn't believe he was going to say it … "Can you give me twenty-four hours? I need to make some calls and check into a few things."

Tears came to Mrs. Pruitt's eyes. "I can arrange that. I know you'll do the right thing."

Flack rubbed his face. "I hope so."

He walked back with the woman and stood in front of the window as Mrs. Pruitt talked. Words like car seat and crib crashed into his brain. *Dear God, what was he doing?*

"Oh, look. She's awake. Come on." Mrs. Pruitt took him by the arm, and the next thing he knew, he was waiting in a small room with several sturdy wooden rockers.

A moment later, Mrs. Pruitt walked into the room with Brooke. The little girl's eyes were huge as she stared at him. "She might not warm up to you right away." The social worker rocked the little girl from side to side. She was beautiful. Dark brown hair and big brown eyes were so like his mother's and sister's.

Flack walked over and reached for the little girl's hand. "Hey, Brooke. Remember me? Uncle Troy?"

Brooke watched him carefully before she leaned toward him and lifted her arms. Mrs. Pruitt's eyebrows rose to her hairline. Flack reached over and awkwardly picked her up from Mrs. Pruitt. He had to jostle her a little bit to get a better grip on her, but he didn't drop her. She didn't weigh anything, and his anger with Trisha's in-laws grew. Fucking troglodytes.

Brooke put her head down on his shoulder and moved her little arm around his neck, almost like she was hugging him. He laid his hand flat on her back and closed his eyes, holding his sister's little girl. She was tiny in his hands, and he lowered his lips to her soft hair. God, how could he raise her? Then again, how could he let someone else?

Brooke coughed a deep harsh cough that rattled her entire body. Once she stopped coughing, the little angel sighed and rested her head against his chest. Dear God, she trusted him. She needed him, and, fuck the world, he'd vow right now to kill anyone who ever hurt her. The baby's breath against his chest delivered waves of protectiveness on the gentle puffs. Brooke was the epitome of those people he'd sworn to protect when he'd joined Guardian. He couldn't turn his back on her. No, it wasn't possible, physically or emotionally.

God, you're going to have to help me because I'm about to do something stupid here. He would not let that little girl go through life alone. He'd fuck it up. That was a guarantee, but maybe with enough help, he could muck his way through it without screwing her up too much. He sat down in the rocker and held his niece. Lord knew he needed help.

His eyes popped open, and he slid his gaze to Mrs. Pruitt. As he smiled, he could see the weight of her worry lift off her. *I have help.* Granted, they weren't experts with kids, but they were masters in adaptability and overcoming obstacles.

FLACK GLANCED at his watch as he slid into his Ferrari. He pulled out his phone and sent a secure text to his crew—Ice, Malice, Harbinger, Reaper, Phoenix, and Valkyrie.

. . .

FLACK: Need immediate assistance, not mission related. Who is in country?

HARBINGER: In Paris. Need me there?

FLACK: No, man. That's cool. Drink some wine for me. I'll call and back brief.

ICE: I'm on my way. ETA two hours.

MALICE: On it. ETA about two hours.

REAPER: In S.D. Can come if you need me.

FLACK: No, but will probably call

REAPER: Anytime

. . .

REAPER WAS the only one of them who had a kid. Flack could imagine the middle of the night calls to Reaper's wife. Lord, he was a fool for thinking he could do it, but damn it, he had to take care of that little girl.

VALKYRIE: You're the only one who would have a crisis on Christmas Day. Can be there in two hours.

GOOD, he really needed a woman's input. Thank God she was in the area.

FLACK: Sorry. Santa dropped a gift on me that can't wait.

VALKYRIE: On our way.

OUR? Oh, that's right, she had a Bravo, or as the rest of the world would call it, a partner now.

Smith. He had yet to meet the man, but all accounts were he was damn good for Valkyrie.

PHOENIX: *We're in town. Be there ASAP.*

THANK GOD. It would take a hive mind to sort out all the shit he needed to do. He put the car into drive and headed home.

CHAPTER 2

*M*alice was the first to arrive. Flack opened the door for his friend, who was carrying several bags of takeout. "Where did you get that? It's Christmas Day."

"Dude, you can always get takeout." Malice entered the dining room and sat the four massive bags on the glass and metal table. "We're meeting in here, right?"

"Probably," Flack admitted. He hadn't thought past getting everyone there. Somehow his brain had been stuck in neutral, or rather the *I can't believe I'm really going to do this* gear.

"Cool. I'm staying the night, by the way. I plan on getting myself a proper Christmas drunk on after we solve whatever problem is bothering you."

"God." Flack ran his hands through his hair. "I'm in a jam, for sure."

Malice turned and looked at him. "Care to tell me what's going on?"

"Flack, you son of a bitch, where are you?" Ice yelled from the front door.

"In the dining room," Flack yelled back.

Ice rounded the corner and laughed. "You got food, too?" Ice lifted three bags. "Chinese. What did you get?"

"Thai." Malice held up his fist, and Ice bumped it.

"Val, Smith, Phoenix, and Aspen are behind me," Ice said as they heard the women's voices in the front room. Phoenix's fiancée was some sort of high-up admin type at Guardian, and her clearance allowed her to know about them. She had to be part of the executive committee, but no one had ever said, and he hadn't asked. It was sufficient that they could be themselves around her.

"In the dining room," Malice called out.

"We brought drinks." Phoenix lifted a case of imported beer.

"And good stuff, too." Val held up two bottles of white wine.

"Woman, that is *not* the good stuff." Ice pointed at her wine.

"What about this?" Smith, or at least Flack assumed the huge man with Val was her partner, Smith, held up a bottle of really old scotch.

"Oh, shit, that is primo hooch! Sparing no expense?" Malice took the bottle from Val's partner. "Never met you, but I know about you. Smith, right?"

"I am." The man nodded, and Malice stuck out his hand. "I'm Malice, that's Ice, and the dick with the problem is Flack." Malice pointed out everyone as he introduced them.

"I'm not a dick," Flack defended himself.

"Yes, you are," both Malice and Ice said at the same time.

"Never mind the fact that Flack is a dick. All lawyers are dicks. We've established this fact many times. Besides, we're celebrating." Valkyrie held up her left hand.

Aspen gasped, grabbed Val's hand, and squealed over the rock dangling off it. "Oh my God! Congratulations."

Flack fell into line to congratulate his friend. By the time they had plates, silverware, and glasses, and everyone settled around the table, he was freaking out and ready to spill on the situation.

"Okay, tell us what got us all here? Not that I'm complaining," Malice said before he shoveled a massive forkful of noodles into his mouth.

"This morning, Smoke showed up at my door." Everyone stopped eating. He had their undivided attention. "My sister Trisha and her husband Steve died right before the Siege. A car accident."

"Damn, man. Sorry to hear that," Ice said the words, and everyone else agreed. He hadn't told anyone; it wasn't like he needed someone to hold his hand. Death happened, and all of them were in the business of dealing with it.

"They had a daughter. She's fourteen months old now. Her grandparents took custody. I was in no position to take a kid; you all understand what I mean. So, anyway, I didn't fight them when they said they'd take her in and apply for custody."

He paused and pushed the small amount of food on his plate away. "The police and social services have been called to their house five times because they weren't taking care of Brooke. She ended up in the hospital. I went to see her, and her case worker said if I didn't take her in, she'd go into foster care."

Malice's head snapped up before he reared back. He shook his head and grated out, "Don't let that happen." The guy had been through hell in the foster system.

Flack held up his hand. "No, I'm not going to let her go into the system. That's why I need your help. I have no idea what I need for a little girl. I have nothing, and I need everything."

Aspen leaned forward. "So, the situation is, you have your niece coming to live with you and no experience taking care of a baby. What medical conditions does she have? I assume something is wrong if she's in the hospital."

"RSV and a badly infected case of diaper rash right now. The RSV has cleared enough that she can come home."

Aspen nodded. "Do you have an online shopping account?"

"Ah, yeah?"

Phoenix's fiancée went into management mode. "Val, you're in charge of clothes, pajamas, diapers, and such. Flack, do you have a car?"

He frowned at the weird question but told her what he had. "Three. The Ferrari, a Lamborghini, and a McClaren."

Smith shook his head. "You can't put a car seat in any of those. You need an SUV."

Malice snorted. "A minivan."

He whipped around and flew his friend the finger. "Fuck you, and hell, no." Flack vetoed that shit right there.

After the laughter receded, Phoenix picked up the conversation again. "We need the best car seat. Smith start researching that." Phoenix pulled out his phone. "I'll find out what type of crib and playpen you need."

"On it." Smith pulled out his phone, too.

"I'll get you an SUV tomorrow." Ice pulled out his phone. "Which ones are the best rated for collision? You got to worry about airbags, crash tests, safety, and shit."

"I'll get the accessories. Flack, we'll need your account password. Fourteen months is old enough to sit in a bathtub, so there's no need for a baby bath." Aspen looked at him expectantly.

Flack rambled off his account name and password.

"What card is on this?" Val asked.

Flack shrugged. "Black."

"Good." She didn't even look up from her

phone as she shopped. "Is she big or small for her age?"

"I don't have a freaking clue, but she was really skinny and so damn small." Flack sighed.

Everyone stopped what they were doing, and Malice growled, "I'll take care of the reason for that for you."

"Troglodytes," Val ground out the word.

Flack shook his head, although he agreed with her. He'd often used that term when talking about his sister's in-laws. They were just ... different. "I'm going to do some digging. Find out what was going on with them."

Malice shrugged. "Offer stands. In the meantime, I'll get you wired for monitors."

"Monitors?" Flack blinked up at him.

"Yeah, dude. You got to be able to keep track of her. If you're down here and she's asleep upstairs, you'll want to keep an eye on her."

"What about weapons?" Aspen looked up from her phone.

"I have enough here to start a war. I don't need more." Flack leaned back. "Most of them are downstairs in the shooting range, though. I might have to bring a few up." Aspen blinked at him, and her mouth fell open. "What? I have to make sure I have a weapon in every room. For protection."

"I think she means, how are you going to secure your weapons, so the baby won't have access to them." Smith didn't smile, but Flack wasn't so sure the guy *wasn't* laughing at him.

"Crap. Yeah, I'll need gun locks." Flack ran his hands through his hair.

"I'll get them, too." Malice offered, still looking at his phone.

Val lifted her head. "Which room are you going to use for hers? I need to measure the windows for curtains."

"Good call." Aspen agreed.

Flack looked toward the stairs. "Ahh …" Shit, he had no idea.

Val grabbed Aspen's hand, and they both stood. "Never mind. We'll go pick it out."

"Wait a minute, Val." Smithson lowered his phone and turned to Flack. "What will you do with your niece when you're working?"

Everyone once again stopped what they were doing and stared at him.

"I'm going to hire a nanny. I can't do this by myself." And that was a task he needed to start working on immediately.

Aspen cocked her head. "What are you going to do until you find a nanny? One who's approved by Guardian?"

Flack dropped his head into his hands. "Pray. Hard. I may have to hire someone from a local service until Guardian can vet someone. I'll just make sure to keep them in the dark."

Ice snorted. "Malice and I will be here for those interviews. I can just see you hiring some long-legged blonde who knows nothing about kids or doesn't have a brain in her head because that's your type." He glanced over to Val. "No offense, doll."

"I have a brain, asshole, so no offense is taken." Val rolled her eyes. "Aspen, can you do any magic concerning obtaining a vetted nanny?"

Aspen thought for a moment. "I know a person who knows a person." She smiled. "But we can do that tomorrow, and it could take a while to push it through. Nobody is at work on Christmas Day. When is your niece supposed to come home with you?"

"Tomorrow afternoon."

"Then we have our timelines, people," Phoenix announced and returned to his phone.

Flack spent the next three hours answering

questions and approving purchases. He finally told them he didn't care what they bought, just to have it delivered by tomorrow afternoon. Especially the crib and car seat. Those were the two things Mrs. Pruitt said that had stuck in his head.

"Val, can you and Smith spend the night tomorrow? Hell, tonight, too, if you want. I need someone to show me the basics."

She blinked at him. "Basics like what?"

Flack lifted his hands in the air and waved them around. "I don't know, things like how to change a diaper. How to wash her hair, stuff like that."

Val blinked. "Dude, I don't know how to do that."

"Dude, I know how to do that." Malice mimicked her from behind them.

Flack spun and asked in disbelief, "You do?"

Malice shrugged, "Yeah, sure. I learned to take care of the little ones when I was in foster care. Not difficult."

"Man, you're a lifesaver." Flack slapped him on the back.

"I'm good with kids. I had three younger brothers and two younger sisters before I died," Ice said as he walked back into the living room.

Smith's head jerked up, and he directed a questioning stare at Val. She put her hand on his arm. "I'll explain later. Long story, and we're too busy right now."

The man stared at her a moment before nodding and returning to searching on his phone.

"I'd have a thousand questions if I overheard that." Flack laughed.

Val made a noncommittal sound. "That's the lawyer in you."

"True, and also the dickishness in you, but we're not picking on you. We're being helpful today," Ice agreed. "Anyway, there are three new Cadillac SUVs on a lot in Alexandria. All with rear and side impact airbags. Do you want black, maroon, or white?"

"I really don't care." Flack rubbed his face, feeling more than just a little overwhelmed. "Can I just give you my credit card?" He was beyond his tipping point.

Ice snorted. "Nah, consider this my Christmas present to you and the kid. I'll pick it up tomorrow morning and bring it here to put in the car seat."

"Dude, you don't have to do that." Flack shook his head.

"She's going to be my niece, too. Me, Uncle

Malice, Uncle Phoenix, Auntie Val … All of us, man, we'll be around her all her life. That little girl is going to be taken care of. Period."

"You'll need to watch some of these videos on the proper way to install the car seat." Smith slid his phone to Flack. "If it's installed improperly, you could hurt or injure her unintentionally."

"Fuck." Flack took the phone and looked up at them. "I'm insane, aren't I?"

"No." The answer came in unison.

"You're doing the right thing for the right reason. We'll all help." Aspen spoke in a very solemn voice. There were nods all around the room.

Flack sighed and looked at the people around him. His support system and, yes, his friends. "You're going to regret that offer because I'm going to need a fuckton of help."

CHAPTER 3

wo Weeks Later:

"ADDISON JEAN, you're going to be late!"

Addy rolled her eyes at her mother's call, which came down the hallway from her childhood bedroom. "I'm not going to be late," she yelled back as she finished combing her hair. She'd let it grow from the cut she'd had while rehabbing, and she could now tuck her brown hair behind her ears. She gave herself a once over. White button-down, black slacks, black jacket. No makeup except lip gloss. She looked professional, presentable, and—she prayed—employable.

"Addison, your Uber is here!" her mother shouted again.

"All right. Coming." She grabbed her briefcase and purse and opened her door.

Her mother stood with her hand lifted to knock on her door. "Oh, I wasn't sure if you heard me."

"I did, thank you." She'd lost hearing in one ear, not both.

"You're not going to eat breakfast, then?"

Addy chuckled. "I don't want to be late." She had an appointment at Compass. They'd just started taking former federal agents for placement services. Normally, they helped transition and place Special Forces and Special Operations personnel into positions like the one she was forced to leave. She stopped and turned. "Momma, I love you. Thank you for worrying, but I don't need you to fuss."

"Your disability pay started last month. Just give it a couple of months and save up."

She smiled and kissed her mom on the cheek. "I can't eat *and* pay rent on my disability, Mom. I'm ready to go to work. If I have to, I'll find something admin based until I can pass the physicals for more strenuous jobs."

"You hate paperwork," her mom said at the same time as her father called from the kitchen, "Keep an open mind!"

"She hates paperwork," her mom yelled back at her dad as Addy headed out the door to her waiting Uber.

Her mom wasn't wrong. She did hate the administrative side of her career. It was the bane of her existence when she worked for the FBI. Thankfully, she was one of the few full-time Special Weapons and Tactics team members. Hell, if she wanted to be stuck in front of a computer screen all day, she could have stayed at the FBI working at a desk. But that wasn't in her genetic code. She had to be active, to move, to go, and to do. Sitting still had never been her strong suit, but with her injuries, she wasn't cleared for fieldwork with the FBI and probably never would be. So she took medical retirement and went home to rehab.

Three months later, she let her apartment lease lapse. Thanks to friends who helped move her possessions, she moved back into her parent's house to save money while she figured out her transition. Everything but her clothes were now in storage, waiting for the next phase of her life. And that was another thing she hated. Waiting.

She flexed her leg, stretching a bit in the back seat of the Uber. After her physical therapy sessions, her replaced knee felt better than her real knee. The hearing loss would be the mountain she had to scale. The homemade explosive the kidnapper had used had messed her over. Flying debris took out her knee, and the percussion stole her hearing. But she'd curled around that little boy, and thankfully, he was spared any injury.

She looked out the window and shook her head, remembering when her father was with her at the hospital. He and her mom took turns staying with her before she was discharged. Addy smiled. On the day after her knee replacement surgery, she'd been feeling sorry for herself, bemoaning her injuries and wondering about her future.

Her dad turned from the window where he'd been listening to her whine. "Addy, let me ask you this. Would you have done anything differently? You knew there was an explosive device, and you knew it could blow, yet you still went in after that little boy. Knowing what you know now, the injuries you received, the hearing loss, would you have done anything differently?"

She stared at her father and let those questions sink in. "No, sir. I would've done the same thing."

"All right, then. Let's focus on the positives. You are alive. That little boy will grow up because of you, and okay, so maybe you won't be able to continue doing what you love. Who's to say you won't find something else that will challenge and excite you?"

Addy glanced down at the resume in her thin profile briefcase. She didn't need a paper copy, Compass had the digital version, but she brought one just in case. As the Uber pulled up to Rio North's company, she drew a deep breath and squared her shoulders. She could do it; a job was out there for her.

Fifteen minutes later, seated in front of her case worker, she had trouble believing that. "Unfortunately, there's a glut of applicants waiting for positions at the moment." Lloyd Rathbone, her assigned case worker, shook his head. "As you probably know, due to the incident this past summer, Guardian, our largest employer, has suspended hiring. We have a tentative date of March first for the freeze to be lifted, which is subject to change. The CIA, ICE, FBI, and Homeland have waitlists as well. We do have corporate positions available. Most require computer, finance, management, or logistical experience."

"I'd prefer something outside an office, but I'll take any interviews I'm qualified for."

Lloyd nodded. "All right, that's the spirit we like to see. Let me pull up the database."

Together, they worked through a list of opportunities and scrubbed it down to five jobs she was qualified to interview for. Lloyd swiveled his screen so she could see the open positions. "I'll print this up for you."

Addy nodded. She glanced at the list. "Wait, there's a Guardian position?" She pointed to the screen.

Lloyd sighed. "Yeah, that's ... Well, I didn't want to bring it up." He shrugged. "You'll see why." Lloyd hit the print button and handed her the paper copy of the job application.

"This is an application for a ... nanny?" She looked up at Lloyd.

"Yep, we received it yesterday. At our staff meeting this morning, we agreed to table this until we could talk to the originator. I don't know what Guardian was thinking about sending the position to us."

Addy looked at the posting again and read aloud, "Qualifications: Self-defense, firearms marksmanship, a Top-Secret clearance, ability to travel for extended periods, current passport, and a degree in psychology."

Lloyd nodded. "It must be working for someone important."

Addy placed the posting on the desk. "I'd like to apply for it."

Lloyd's head almost snapped off his neck when he whipped around to look at her. "What?"

"Listen, these positions ..." she waved at the others listed, "are good. I'll interview for all of them just to make sure I get a job, but ..." *being at a keyboard all day would suck the life out of me,* "I'm good with kids and meet all the qualifications listed." Except she'd need an upgraded clearance, but no disqualifiers would prevent that from happening.

Lloyd thumped his fingers on the desk for a moment and flicked his gaze from the computer to her. "I'll need to get clearance to release this post. Give me a second?"

"Sure." Addy leaned back in her chair and watched as Lloyd left his office. She placed all six job positions on the desk and examined each one. Her eyes kept going back to the position for Guardian.

Lloyd was back a few moments later. "Ms.

Wilson, this is the owner of our company, Rio North."

Addy stood up and shook the man's hand. "A pleasure to meet you. You're kind of a legend." The man had established the first-ever clearing house for Spec Ops personnel looking for employment outside the service. He was now taking on transitioning government employees, too.

The man laughed. "No, just a guy doing what he can. I wanted to assure you that this isn't our typical posting. I made an exception for this particular post since it came from the highest echelons of Guardian. We believe our candidates, all of them, are qualified for positions higher than this posting."

"I understand, but since we're being honest here, I'd go insane sitting in front of a computer all day. Until the hiring doors open at Guardian and I can apply for a field position with their Domestic Operations division, I'm more than happy to do something like this. If I do a good enough job, maybe the parents will give me a recommendation." She shrugged. "Regardless, I'd like to apply for it and the others I qualify for."

Rio extended his hand. "Then I wish you the

best on your interviews. Lloyd will set them up for you. Good luck."

"Thank you." Addy shook his hand and sat down with Lloyd. The man picked up his phone and started to schedule her interviews.

lack picked up Brooke and headed downstairs. The diaper rash was better, and damn, could the girl blow out the bottom of a diaper. "Glad it was your turn. That smelled like a nuclear mess." Malice laughed at him when he put Brooke on the couch between Malice and Ice. The little girl immediately scooted up in Malice's lap and flirted with Ice.

"Dude, you're going to have to hire armed guards for her at school." Ice hid his face and played peek-a-boo with Brooke.

"No doubt. How many interviews do we have today?"

"Three." Ice grabbed his phone. "Two from the temp service and one from the Guardian posting.

Let's see. The first one is twenty-three, her name is Destiny, and she loves children, puppies, and long walks on the beach."

Malice snorted a laugh, causing Brooke to giggle. "It does not say that."

"I sh—shoot you not." Ice made a face at Brooke and handed the phone to Malice.

"Soot." Brooke mimicked the word and smiled when all of them laughed.

"Yeah, the second one is Brittany. She's twenty-two, loves to travel, play with children, and cook nutritious meals." Malice rolled his eyes. "Are they trying to be Miss America or something?"

"I couldn't tell you." When Flack flopped down into the armchair, Brooke immediately reached for him. Ice picked her up and passed her over. He would have never made it the last two weeks without Malice and Ice. The house looked like a tornado had hit it, but they were coping. Once he'd hired a nanny, he'd get the house settled. That had to be soon because even though Mrs. Pruitt had visited several times since Brooke had come to live with him, a new case worker was being assigned now that he'd applied for guardianship. Thank God for his crew. They watched Brooke while he completed the paperwork to satisfy the courts.

Flack was sleep-deprived, and he fucking needed a shower, but he was dealing. "What's the name of the one Guardian sent?"

"Addison Wilson." Ice read the application. "Dude, she's—" The doorbell rang, stopping him.

Flack stood and handed Brooke back to Ice. He went to the door and opened it. The girl standing at the door was blonde, wearing enough makeup to go clubbing, and her skirt was almost long enough to cover her ass. Almost. "Hi, I'm Destiny. Nice place." She lifted her phone and took a snap of herself smiling.

"Yeah. Good to meet you." Flack was not impressed. "Come in."

Destiny stepped through the boxes of stuff his crew had ordered for Brooke that he hadn't had the time or energy to open. She tiptoed around the cartons and containers like she was walking through a dog park with land mines everywhere. Destiny smiled as she was introduced to Malice and Ice.

"So, are you a tripod?" She sat down on the edge of the seat.

"Am I a what?" Flack grabbed Brooke and sat down with her.

"Not that it matters." The woman smiled. "What's the salary?"

Flack put Brooke down, and Ice moved to guarantee she didn't fall as she toddled between the coffee table and the couches. "Let's discuss your qualifications first, shall we?"

Destiny shook her head. "No, that's a waste of time if the pay isn't enough. I don't want to, like, be a wagie."

"A wagie?" Malice asked.

She clicked her tongue and sighed as she rolled her eyes. "Yeah, a person who gets paid hourly. Lives paycheck to paycheck. A *wagie*. I'm not into that, and I have bills to pay, so, like, how much is the salary?"

Flack stood up. "All right, Destiny. Thank you for coming."

She blinked and looked up at him. "What?"

"I'm ending the interview. Thank you for coming over. I won't be calling you." Flack motioned toward the door.

"Rude much?" the woman sniped as she passed Flack and headed to the door.

"Only to people like you." He closed the door after her and dropped onto the frosted glass. "Tell me it wasn't just me."

Malice grabbed Brooke and swung her into the air. "Flack, I'd *do* Destiny all day, every day, but I wouldn't let my niece within a city block of that self-centered airhead."

Ice agreed. "I have her number, Malice. Take her to a five-star restaurant, and you'll be set for the weekend."

"That's an idea, but I'll pass. I prefer my women more mature."

"And taller," Ice added.

"She's your type, isn't she, Ice?" Malice spun Brooke around as he asked.

"Oh, he— heck yeah, but too materialistic. Which are words I never thought I'd say." He grabbed Brooke and gave her a raspberry on the tummy. "You're changing me, my lady." Brooke laughed and grabbed his hair when he bent down and blew another on her stomach.

Flack sighed. "What time is the next one coming?"

"At two. The last one at four," Ice said between raspberries.

"Then let's get this girl some lunch and down for a nap." Flack wanted to shower and shave before the next woman showed up.

Lunch was a production as none of them could

cook worth a shit. Flack cut up a banana, and Ice
dabbed a bit of peanut butter on each slice. Malice
tore small pieces of rotisserie chicken up and
placed them on her highchair. Flack toasted some
bread as Ice severely damaged an avocado trying to
get the seed out. Didn't matter because the slimy
thing got smushed on the toast. Brooke loved
smearing the green slime all over the deck of her
highchair. Flack opened another can of mixed
veggies and drained them. He nuked the carrots,
peas, and corn for a couple of seconds, then
dropped a warmed mound onto her highchair.

"Where's her sippy cup?" Flack started lifting
dirty dishes out of the sink, looking for it.

"Refrigerator?" Malice suggested.

Flack opened the door and moved shit around.
Between their takeout food containers and
Brooke's stuff, the fridge was trashed and disorga-
nized. "There you are." He opened the cap to see
what was in it. "Damn." Whatever it was, Brooke
wouldn't drink it. He turned on the hot water and
found some soap. "So, we're down to Brittany and
the Guardian application, right?"

"Yeah," Ice said as he gave Brooke another piece
of carrot to eat. "I was going to tell you about the
Guardian chick."

The doorbell rang, and Flack groaned. "Not another delivery? People, we agreed to stop buying until we can find ground zero." Flack flung the soap off his hands and marched to the front door. He whipped it open and stopped short. A woman about his age stood on the steps. She wore black slacks, a white button-down, and a black suit jacket. "Oh, damn, sorry, I thought you were a delivery person."

"Sorry." She looked behind him. "I think you're set in that department."

Flack laughed. "You have no idea. Can I help you?"

The woman smiled, and damn, she had a nice one. Her big brown eyes sparkled, and she lit up his front porch like a roman candle lights up the night sky on the Fourth of July. "Hi, I'm Addison Wilson. I have an appointment at noon today with Mr. Troy Masters regarding a position as a nanny?"

Troy stuck out his hand and noticed the soap on it. He wiped it on his jeans, then shook her hand. "I'm Troy. We thought your appointment was at two, or was it four?"

The woman shook her head. "No, sir. My

confirmation slip from the agency says noon. Today." She flashed her phone at him.

"Swell. Well, we're in here." Troy opened the door wider.

"Does your wife work for Guardian as well?" the woman asked as she walked into the house. Flack saw her take in the mess, but she didn't react. Score one for the brunette.

"I'm not married. My sister passed, and I've just taken over guardianship of my niece." He motioned into the kitchen. "My co-workers and I are trying to keep our heads above water until we can find someone to help."

Addison walked into the kitchen and extended her hand to Ice. "Addy."

"Hey. Call me Ice."

The woman nodded and turned to Malice. "Addy. Nice to meet you."

"Thank God, a *real* person." Malice wiped his hands on his jeans. "Call me Malice."

Addy looked from one to the other and then back at Flack. "And you go by?"

"Flack, but Troy is better around Brooke," he admitted.

"All right. So, is this the little angel?" Addy

walked across the kitchen floor and bent down by the highchair. "Hey, sweetheart."

Brooke grabbed a piece of avocado toast and squished it through her fingers. "Toast." Or Brooke's equivalent of the word came out of a full mouth.

Addy laughed and looked around. She stood carefully before grabbing a paper towel and wetting it at the sink overflowing with dirty dishes. She talked to Brooke the entire time. "Did you know you have avocado in your hair?" She moved back and wiped the green slime out of Brooke's hair. "I'll tell you a secret, it's supposed to be great for a hair conditioner, but you should probably wait until you're just a bit older."

Addy wiped Brooke's hands and then her face. "Does she take a bottle still, or is she on a sippy cup?"

Flack was jolted out of watching Addy with Brooke and grabbed the one he'd been cleaning. The woman was a natural with Brooke, and his princess was happy to let Addy take care of her. Damn, that was something. He really liked that. "Sorry, that was why my hands were soapy when you rang the bell." He finished washing out the cup and filled it with filtered water from the refrigerator.

Addy took it and picked Brooke up from the highchair. "There you go." She turned to Flack. "I know you're not prepared for my interview, but since I'm here, should we continue?"

Flack nodded. "Of course. Come into the front room, and we'll talk."

"Do you want me to take Brooke?" Malice asked as he and Ice followed them into the living room.

"No, I've got her." Addy bounced Brooke a bit. "Don't I, sweet girl?" Brooke smiled and dropped her sippy cup, but Addy caught it deftly. "Whoopsie."

Once they were all seated, Flack leaned forward. "I'm sorry I haven't looked at your CV. Can you briefly explain your qualifications and why you're applying for the job?"

"I recently left the FBI. I was in charge of Team Three, Special Weapons, and Tactics. We were deployed on a kidnapping, a barricaded suspect call. The suspect had improvised a homemade explosive. A four-year-old boy was going to be killed if we didn't act. As the ranking member and team lead, I ordered my team to stand down and went in after him. The device went off, but I was able to shield the child. My knee was torn to pieces, and they replaced it. I lost my hearing in my left ear. The hearing issue prevents me from working on the Special Weapons and Tactics team. I hate paperwork, so I took a medical retirement from the agency. I have provided a list of references, and Compass has vetted me as qualified for this position."

"And your knee?" Malice asked.

"Fully functional but a little bit weak at this point. Physical therapy is over. Now it's time for me to hit the gym and strengthen it." Addy answered the question while letting Brooke pull on her suit jacket. "I have a bachelor's degree in psychology, a secret clearance, and an upgrade to Top Secret will not be an issue. I'm an expert marksman with the M-9 and the M-4. As far as self-defense, I've learned from the best. For the short term, that would be the only lim-fac as I'm still strengthening my knee."

Flack was kind of falling in love with the woman. She handled Brooke with ease that wasn't faked, and she spoke his language. "The limiting factor isn't an issue at this point. Our work for Guardian is slow at the moment due to the Siege."

Addy put Brooke on her knee, presumably the good one, and bounced her. Flack watched how she handled his niece. He was impressed and a bit jealous. He only hoped he'd get that confident with her.

"Is that what you're calling it internally? The Siege?"

What? Oh ...

"It is," Malice acknowledged.

"That fits. We watched and responded to relieve the D.C. cops after the first forty-eight hours. Unbelievable."

"It was." Flack cleared his throat. "About the salary ..."

"I saw what was advertised and I'm very happy with what you've offered. Room and board are provided, correct?" Addy looked up at him.

Flack nodded. "Yes. I need around-the-clock help. Although I'll give you downtime if you get the position. Unless I'm traveling for work. Then I'll reimburse you as appropriate."

"I'm not worried about that. I'd rather be busy. If I need to go somewhere, I can take her. You have a car seat and a vehicle I can use?"

"Yeah. Brand new," Flack said as Ice chuckled from where he and Malice were listening.

"Then downtime isn't a big issue." She shrugged, seeming nonplused that his crew was part of the conversation. She shot him a glance before she made a face at Brooke, causing the little girl to laugh. "Look, I'll be honest. I hate pushing paper, and the three positions I've interviewed for have offered me jobs. It looks to me like you *need* me to work with you. They *want* me to push paper. I'd rather deal with dirty diapers and fussy babies any day. But you're not fussy, are you?" she spoke to Brooke, and the girl smiled at her.

Flack nodded. "That sounds …"

"Perfect," Malice finished for him.

"What he said," Ice added.

Addy laughed. "Do they live here?"

"Well, since I took custody of Brooke, yes. But they have homes of their own." Flack laughed.

"A good team is irreplaceable." Addy nodded. "It's hard to find the right person to jive with all the personalities of a crew. I get that. So," she stood up and handed Brooke to Flack, "unless you have any other questions, I'll let you guys discuss the pros and cons of hiring me."

Flack adjusted Brooke on his hip. "I do have

one question." Addy turned and looked at him. "When can you start?" He was not letting that woman out of the house without offering her the job.

"Fuck, yeah," Malice said, then slapped his hand over his mouth, immediately glancing in Brooke's direction.

Addy smiled and put her hands on her hips, looking around the disaster area that used to be his house. "Give me a couple of hours to pack. I'll be back as soon as possible."

Flack extended his hand, and relief flooded over him. "Thank God, and welcome aboard."

She shook his hand. "I look forward to it."

CHAPTER 5

"Mom, you wouldn't believe how badly those three guys need help. I mean, they were managing because that little girl was happy, and she had them wrapped around her little fingers, but Lord, that house is a disaster." She folded her shirt into her suitcase as her mom folded her jeans, placing them in a different case.

"How old is the girl?"

Addy stood up and frowned. "You know, I didn't ask. She's probably a year or a little more. Her teeth were mostly through, and she was drooling like crazy, so maybe her molars? I don't know for sure, but she was eating solid food. She was so sweet, and it looked like they were trying to feed her a balanced meal, but good Lord, the mess she was making." Addy laughed. "Mom, I don't think any of them know what a bib is or how to use it."

Her mom smiled and packed some more of her clothes. "Are you going to be fulfilled doing this?"

Addy shrugged. "I'm thinking of it as a stepping stone. Guardian isn't hiring for several months, maybe longer. And we both know I'd die a thousand deaths at those other companies doing mindless paperwork. I can build a little gym of sorts in my room and rehab when the baby is sleeping. I make a great salary, damn good money according to the paperwork."

"What does he do for Guardian?" Her mother moved to her closet. "Suits?"

"I don't think so. It didn't look like formal attire was required."

"I'll pack one, just in case."

"That works. As far as what he does, I believe he works on a team. Like a SEAL Team, but they work for Guardian."

"That's why he'd be away for months."

"Yep."

Her mother stopped with her suit half-folded. "Then you need to make sure there's someone identified to take care of that baby if he doesn't make it back from one of those trips."

"Yeah, not exactly in my area of responsibility." She chuckled. "But I get what you mean."

"You feel safe staying in this man's house?" Her mother sat down on the bed.

She stopped packing and sat next to her mom. "I do. I know you worry, but, Mom, of all of your children, who would you want in an alley fight with you?"

Her mother laughed and leaned into her. "You, of course. Beth and Carol are girly girls."

"I can take care of myself, and I'll take good care of that little girl because you taught me how. Thankfully, all those babysitting jobs have come in handy. I'll bring her over when we get settled so you can meet her." Addy saw the happiness that showed in her mother's smile. Beth and Carol, her younger sisters, were married, but neither had yet started a family. Her mother was seriously jonesing for a grandbaby to love on.

"Oh, I'd love that. Let's finish getting you packed so you're ready when Pete picks you up. I'm sorry your dad took the car into the city."

"No worries, Mom. Pete and I are on good

terms." Sort of … maybe. Addy grabbed another stack of t-shirts. "He can wait a minute or ten."

* * *

FLACK FINISHED STACKING the boxes in the foyer. Just that minor improvement seemed to take a joint effort between the three men. "Dude, what room will she stay in?" Ice asked from the top of the stairs.

Flack rubbed his neck. "The one next to Brooke's."

"It's full of my crap," Ice mumbled. "Good thing I'm packing up."

"Say what now?" Flack grabbed hold of the banister as he looked up at his friend.

"Yeah, dude, with the nanny here, you don't need Malice and me. We've been packing while the kiddo sleeps."

Flack nodded. It made sense for them to get back to their lives. "Man, I couldn't have done this shit without you."

Ice nodded. "It takes a village."

"What the hell does that mean?" Flack asked as he walked up the stairs.

"You can't raise a kid by yourself," Ice

answered. "It takes a village. Something my mom used to say when she babysat for others."

Flack sat down at the top of the stairs, and Ice sat beside him and said, "You got this, man."

"I'm not so sure, but I'm a hell of a lot closer to juggling it now. Appreciate the assist." Flack could admit when he needed help, that was for damn sure.

"Aww, don't you two look like you lost your puppy or something," Malice said from where he leaned against the wall at the end of the hallway.

"Dude, I was going to say thank you to you, too." Flack laughed.

"Whatever." Malice brushed him off. "Go take a shower. We'll finish packing while the princess is sleeping."

"Shit, that sounds like a deal." He stood, walked over to Malice, and offered his hand. "Seriously, thank you."

Malice took his hand and pulled him into a quick hug. "Yeah, like I said, shower." The guy slapped Flack on the back and walked away.

He glanced over at Ice, who shrugged. "He doesn't know how to do emotion too well." The doorbell rang, chiming through the house.

"Is she here already?" Flack looked at his watch.

"Nah, that's probably your two o'clock. I'll go break the news to her." Ice stood up and trotted down the stairs. At the bottom, he turned and looked back up. "Maybe get her number, too."

Flack shook his head and headed to his bedroom. He glanced around the house that had been immaculate until two weeks ago. It looked like an online shopping orgasm had spewed across his house, leaving trails of boxes all over. He stopped outside Brooke's room and quietly opened the door before tiptoeing in and checking to make sure she was okay. Her little jaws moved in a sucking motion. He looked at all the empty bottles on her dresser. Mrs. Pruitt had said she still took a bottle at bedtime, so they gave her one for her naps and at night. Sooner or later, they would run out of new bottles Val and Aspen had washed.

He moved out of the room, careful not to trip on any of the boxes before heading to his room. He closed the door behind him and looked longingly at his bed. He hadn't slept a full night since Brooke came to stay with him. At first, it was because she woke up crying, then it was because she didn't, so he'd freak out and go in and check on her.

He walked into his bathroom and turned on the shower. How stupid was that? Lord, how did parents do it? Some had multiple kids. One was enough to worry him to death. He dropped his head back under the water and grabbed a bar of soap.

"What's next?" he spoke to himself as he soaped up.

Well, the first thing was to organize the house so that when the new case worker showed up, it didn't look like a frat house after rush week. Next, he'd have Addy make a list of the things she needed that they hadn't bought. Fuck, he needed to clean out the takeout from the fridge and find out what kind of food Addy suggested for Brooke. He'd started an online grocery shopping cart that delivered daily. He'd give Addy access to that and his Prime account so she could order whatever she needed or wanted. Getting Addy settled would get Brooke settled, and then maybe he could breathe. Flack rinsed off, stepped out of the shower, and grabbed a towel. Laundry. Fuck, he needed to gather the dirty clothes and get the laundry service to come by and pick them up. Same-day service was a thing for laundries, right? Hell, he had no clue.

Flack brushed his teeth as he continued his list of must-dos. He needed to go in and see Smoke and call Anubis to let work know he was still alive. Ice and Malice had already checked back in and were ready for assignments, but Guardian hadn't had any need for them yet.

He slipped into some jeans and a t-shirt before he finger-combed his hair and glanced at himself in the mirror. He had his mom's skin tone and his dad's stature. He and his father had both been linebackers at the University of Michigan, where they'd obtained their under-graduate degrees. His father went to Harvard Law, but Flack went to Yale Law. It was a rivalry that they'd had fun with. His dark brown hair, brown eyes, and year-round bronzed skin were gifts from his mom's genetics. She was a beautiful woman his father had met and fallen instantly in love with when he was on a business trip in Brazil. He'd asked her to marry him one week after meeting her, and she'd said yes. The rest, as they said, was history.

Flack headed downstairs but popped in on Brooke to see if she was still sleeping. As he came out of her room, he saw Malice with his duffle bag heading downstairs. Ice was already in the foyer. "Well, Flack, do you think you can handle the princess for a couple of hours, or do you want us to stay?" Malice dropped his duffle on the imported marble flooring.

"I think I can handle it. I appreciate it. If either of you needs anything, you only have to call. Now that Addy is in the picture, I'll be there."

Ice snorted. "Dude, this was probably the weirdest call for assistance we'll ever have." His friends picked up their bags and walked out the front door with him. "Remember, Addy has skills. She can kick your ass," Ice said, chuckling as he tossed his bag into the back of his car.

"And outshoot you," Malice added.

"You're both full of shit." Flack laughed with them, then watched as they backed out of the long drive and pulled away. He went back inside and looked around at the total devastation. Damn. He'd start in the kitchen.

Flack found the monitor and turned it up before unloading the dishwasher. After loading it again and turning it on, he worked on the pots and pans they'd used. Once he'd scrubbed one frying pan for five minutes, he tossed it in the garbage. It wasn't worth saving if he couldn't chip the shit off the pan after a few minutes.

He'd just started emptying take-out containers from the fridge when he heard Brooke squawk.

Flack headed upstairs. She was usually good for a couple of minutes, but he'd been diligent about changing her now that the sores on her little butt had mostly healed. When he'd first seen what was going on with the diaper rash, he'd almost gagged. How long did a baby have to sit in their own mess to get sores that bad? He hated Trisha's in-laws more every time he changed her and listened to her cry because of the discomfort of the sores when he cleaned her up.

He opened the door and saw her standing on the mattress, holding the crib rail. "Hey, my little beauty. How are you?" He picked her up and took her straight to the changing table. She smiled up at him when he laid her down. God, how could anyone neglect an angel baby like her? Brooke gurgled, squealed, and babbled her nonsense talk. Although she said a few words, he could have sworn she'd said dada once or twice. That sobered him. She didn't have a dada. That was going to suck for her, wasn't it? He'd do his best to make sure she didn't miss her parents too much. She was his now. His to worry about, to care for, and to love.

Flack made faces at her and gave her a raspberry on her belly when he was done changing her.

He put her feet back in the fluffy pajamas she was wearing. Although Val had bought her a shitload of clothes, keeping her in something he didn't have to wrangle over her head and try to button up was easier. The little girl twisted into pretzels whenever he tried to find a button or a snap. Velcro and zippers were his friends right now.

Flack shook his head. Velcro and zippers, not poison darts and weapons. Not research and information. Damn, he'd morphed into someone he didn't recognize, and at times, he wasn't sure if that was a good thing or not. He wanted to work; he wanted to continue to do what he did for Guardian, but that *want* pulled him away from what he *needed* to do. He needed to guarantee the angel was taken care of. Damn, sometimes getting pinched between a rock and a hard place had zero wiggle room and made you as uncomfortable as fuck.

Brooke finally let him get the pajamas on, and he felt like he'd scaled a mountain. At least he'd reached the top. Sort of. "Let's go downstairs and have a snack. Does that sound good? Sure, it does." He pulled out old pizza boxes and take-out containers while Brooke smooshed more avocado toast and ate some small pieces of chicken and bits of banana. He'd just dumped both massive black bags into the garage when the doorbell rang.

He grabbed Brooke out of the highchair without wiping off her hands. She grabbed his shirt and left smears of avocado and banana on his fresh t-shirt, but Flack shrugged it off. He was over caring what he looked like. As long as Brooke was healthy and happy, he was fine.

He opened the door, expecting to see Addy. Instead, a tall, rail-thin woman stood at the door. The look of disdain that dripped off her set him on edge, and not much did that. Every protective gene in his body flared to life. The woman, whoever she was, radiated hostility.

"Can I help you?"

"Mr. Troy Masters?" the woman asked. He nodded. "I'm Bridget Harper, your new case worker. I've come to do an inspection of your home."

Flack stepped in front of the woman as she moved to enter his house. "I want to see some identification, and what child protective regulation are you citing for an unannounced visit?"

The woman rolled her eyes and produced a badge showing her as a CPS social worker. "I have every right to make surprise visits on placed children."

Flack cocked his head at her. "According to what I've read, you have every right to do an inspection if you suspect neglect. Have you received a complaint? Does she look unhealthy or unhappy to you?"

"Mr. Masters." The woman pulled out her notebook and whipped a pen from her bag. "Are you refusing me entrance to your home?"

"Mrs. Harper, was it?"

"It's *Ms.* Harper." The woman enunciated the word.

"I'm telling you that I'm a lawyer and know my rights. I don't have to allow you into the house if it isn't a good time for me unless you have a court order granting you access. Do you have a court order?"

The woman's nose went farther into the air. "No."

"Do you have any complaints concerning my custody of my niece?"

"No, but I can't understand why you're refusing access."

Flack smiled at her politely and balanced Brooke on his arm as he spoke to the evil spirit inhabiting the stick figure at his door. "You don't have to understand it. Just accept the fact that I'm not granting it. Please do call. I'm sure you have my number and can arrange a more convenient time for your inspection. Now, if you'll excuse me, we need to wash up. You interrupted snack time."

He shut the door behind him and sighed dramatically. Brooke smiled and patted his face with her slimy hands. "Thank you, sweetie, just what Uncle Troy needed." That monster of a woman would play hell with his process of guardianship. He could feel it in the pit of his gut. But she had a hell of a fight in front of her. Brooke was his niece, his princess, and that twig of a demon wouldn't take her away from him. He had the law on his side, and he'd use everything he had to keep her. He glanced at his home and the disaster surrounding him. Damn, still, he needed help. "Addy, please hurry up."

CHAPTER 6

"Thanks for giving me a ride over, Pete," Addy said as they pulled into the driveway of Troy Masters' home.

"No problem. You know, as soon as you told me who you were working for, I ran him." Pete put the car into Park.

Addy rolled her eyes. "You did not."

Pete hmphed and got out of his truck when she opened her door. He walked to the back and opened the tailgate.

"I did. There's nothing on this guy. Like absolutely nothing." Pete pulled one of her suitcases out of the back of the truck and held onto it when she went to pick it up.

"Pete, he's Guardian. *Elite* Guardian. Leave this

alone before you get slapped for using resources improperly." She yanked the handle out of his hand.

"Ads, seriously, you know this is killing me. You need to come back to work with us. We need to fix us." Pete slipped in front of her and put his hands on her shoulders.

She looked up at him. "Pete, we tried and failed. This, what was between us, isn't going to work because I will not kowtow to you, and you have to be in charge of everything. I'm done fighting with you, I'm done arguing, and I'm done talking about it. Go out and find a little woman who'll be your yes girl. That's not me, and it will never be me."

She reached for her second suitcase, but he moved so she couldn't reach it. Had she known the situation would devolve into yet another dialog of their failed relationship, she wouldn't have canceled her Uber. It was cold out, and she hadn't worn her winter coat, packing it instead. "Pete, come on, I'm cold, and I need to get inside."

"Ads, the sex was great." Pete pushed her hair back behind her ear in a possessive move. She sighed. "Pete, the sex was okay *at best*, but you can't base a relationship on sex alone." It wasn't great, at least not for her. She shivered, and it wasn't because of any sexual tension.

"Then go out with me again. Now that you're out of the agency, maybe we won't clash as hard?"

"I'm just starting this job. I don't think so." She moved around him and pulled out her second suitcase.

He stepped in front of her again. "Next month, then. I'll pick you up. We'll have dinner." He tipped her head up to look at him.

Addy rolled her eyes. "Fine, next month. Call me first."

Pete dropped a kiss on her before she knew what he was doing. She moved quickly to the left and almost fell. Pete reached for her, but she jerked her arm out of his grasp. "Thank you for the ride, Pete. I need to go inside. My employer is waiting for me." She nodded to the door.

Pete turned and did a double take at the man standing at the door. That was exactly what Addy had thought when she'd seen him. He was at least six-feet-four-inches tall and built like a mountain. His dark eyes and hair and all those muscles were distracting in a wonderful way. But she knew how to keep things professional, and she'd never cross that line.

"Everything all right?" Troy called from where he stood, holding Brooke. The little girl's dark brown hair was standing on end like a lion's mane.

She waved. "Be right there."

"Who the fuck is this guy?" Pete hissed. "I thought you were caring for some old guy's niece."

"I didn't tell you that. You assumed, as usual. Thanks for the ride. I'll talk to you later." She tugged the suitcases down the driveway toward the house.

"One month, Ads," Pete called after her.

She didn't even try to reply. When he called next month, she'd blow him off. Sometimes it was just easier to put distance between Pete and his controlling manipulations. She reached the expansive porch, which blocked the cold wind, and stopped. "Sorry, an old friend was trying to become relevant again."

Troy, or Flack as his friends called him, nodded while staring at Pete, who was backing out of the drive. "Are you anticipating any problems with him?"

She snorted. "Lord, no. He's hoping for something that will never happen."

"Well, then, how about we trade? You take her, and I'll take your suitcases to your room."

"That sounds like a deal. Come here, butter-cup." She held out her arms and wiggled her fingers at the gorgeous little girl.

Brooke played coy for about two seconds before leaning over toward Addy. "See, you remember me, right?"

As she followed Troy into the house, the heat enveloped her. "Oh, man, this is bigger than I remember." She glanced over at the far wall where all the online shopping boxes were stacked, making the foyer seem much larger.

"Yeah, well, you didn't see me at my best this morning. I have a list of things I must do before Social Services shows up again."

"Excuse me?" Why were social services at his house?

"A new case worker showed up unannounced today and wanted to do an inspection."

"Can they do that? I haven't looked at any CPS regulations, but that doesn't sound right." She followed him to the stairs and held Brooke with one hand, grasping the handrail with the other just in case her knee went wonky. It hadn't given out in a long time, but she wasn't taking chances with the baby.

"No, they can't unless there's a complaint about

the child's safety or they have a court order. She had neither, and Brooke was in my arms when I answered the door. Granted, she was covered in avocado again, but she was happy, and Ms. Harper knew I had every right to tell her to call and schedule a better time."

"All right, then, we need to kick the organizational effort into high gear." She watched as Troy opened a bedroom door.

"This will be your room. There are fresh linens in the hall closet. Ice was using this room. I changed out the towels in the bathroom for you, which is over there," he shared, pointing to another door in the room. "It's an en suite, so you have privacy. The closet is over here. If you need anything I don't have, I'll give you access to my online shopping account, and you can order whatever you need."

"Thanks, but this looks more than adequate." It was massive and beautiful. More space than she'd had in her entire D.C. apartment. Returning to the hall, she opened the door next to her room and was met by a wall of boxes. "Well, this will need to be fixed, won't it?" She laughed when Brooke clapped her hands. "I think you like that idea, too, huh?"

"Sorry, you can get in this way." Troy walked to the next door and opened it.

Addy blinked, then laughed. "It looks like a pink unicorn barfed rainbow sparkles and glitter ruffles in here."

Flack walked in and nodded his head. "My friends, some you didn't meet today, helped order stuff for her. I had nothing."

Addy took in the array of boxes stacked around the room's four walls. "Well, now you have enough to start your own department store."

"Yeah." Troy shook his head. "I don't know where I'm going to put it all."

"Why don't we see what you have now, and if we don't need everything that was ordered, you can send it back? I'd suggest stacking the returns in the garage until they send a semi to get it all."

"There's a lot of stuff." Troy nodded. "I think we all panicked," he said with a rueful smile.

"Yeah, I think mass hysteria would be a better categorization. Okay, so that box is a play and pack. Open that up, and she'll be safe to amuse herself while we go through boxes."

"Look, you didn't hire on to do this. You're supposed to watch her, not put my life in order. Now that you're here, I can start sorting this sh—

stuff out." Troy moved several stacks of boxes to reach the play and pack that she'd glimpsed behind them.

"Good catch, and as long as she's happy playing by herself, I'll help." Addy watched as Troy unboxed the playpen.

"It won't open." He tugged on the legs trying to separate them.

"Is there a button?" Addy suggested.

"What like an umbrella?" Troy lifted the white tubes and turned them around, inspecting them. "No."

"Maybe a hook?" She suggested an alternative and smiled at the childlike consternation on his face. God, he was sexy and cute. Whoa, girl. Stop right there.

"Nope. Just these and this." He extended a tube, and it made a click. Troy looked at her. "That sounded like a claymore activating."

She blinked. "No kidding. And isn't it crazy that we both thought that?" Addy laughed. "Where are the instructions?"

"The destructions are ..." Troy opened the box and looked in. "Not in here."

"Did you call them destructions?"

"Well, yeah. My father used to call them that."

Troy spun the metal tubbing, and Brooke laughed, reaching for it.

"No, not yet, sweetie. Uncle Troy needs to fix it first." Addy redirected her hand and bounced the baby. "Check on the back of the box. Maybe the instructions are printed there."

Troy flipped the box over. "Easy opening." He looked at her. "They lied about that."

Addy rolled her eyes. Yeah, he was cute and sexy. Lord, she was in trouble. "Keep reading."

"Simply press ... oh." Troy put the metal bars down and pressed a silver disk. The metal released and snapped into a square. The bottom formed, and the mesh walls went up. Troy looked at the box again and then latched the sides into place. He laid the pad down on the floor of the playpen. "Cool. I'm smarter than a playpen."

Addy laughed. "I would say that you're on equal terms about now." She sat Brooke in the pen and handed her several age-appropriate toys that were unboxed and scattered about the room.

"So, when social services come, what exactly will they be looking for?"

"According to Mrs. Pruitt, safety is the priority. I bought locks for all the weapons in the house. Most of them are secured downstairs in the shooting range, but I have several around the house."

Addy stopped opening a random box and looked over at him. "You have an indoor shooting range?"

Troy held up a box, totally ignoring her question … because … "I'm going to kill someone." He turned it around to show her a breast pump.

Addy laughed until she cried. "Oh, God, I love your friends."

"Yeah, well, I'm not so sure I do." He tossed it back in the box he took it out of and walked the box to the door. "Returns will go in the hall. And yes, downstairs, there's a shooting range and a gym. I'll show you where everything is after she goes to bed for the night." Troy picked up another box and opened it. "Diapers." He pulled out five huge packages.

"Those we'll keep. Set them next to the changing table, please." Addy motioned to the most logical place for them. They unboxed and worked together, taking breaks to amuse Brooke until the little girl fussed in earnest. Addy picked her up. "Okay, sweetheart. You've been a champ. How about a diaper change and then some dinner?"

Troy flattened another box and added it to the

stack of cardboard that would go out for recycling. "Wow, that didn't take long." He grabbed the entire stack of cardboard. "I'll get this out of here and then start the process of returning those things."

Addy reached for the wipes and unfastened the little girl's diaper. "Oh, wow." She cleaned the baby. "What happened here?" The scars were unexpected.

"Her grandparents didn't change her enough," Troy grunted as he went through the door with all the boxes. "You should have seen it when she first came to stay with me. That's only part of the reason I'm taking care of her."

"Part?"

"Yeah. They gave me some medicated cream to use. It's on the changing table."

Addy looked down at the sweet little girl. "Well, darling, it seems like you've had a rough patch." She talked to the baby as she changed her. "I think you'll be fine. Your Uncle Troy is head over heels in love with you already. Yes, he is." She fastened the baby's pajamas and looked around the room. "We need to do something with that wild hair of yours. Addy picked up Brooke, and they bounced over to the dresser and went through the drawers. "Okay, so I'm going to thank whatever uncle shopped for this." She sat Brooke down on the floor with her and used a soft brush to detangle her hair and brush it out. Then she gathered it all and clipped it into a crazy ponytail on the top of her head. "There you go. Out of your eyes and not as wild." Brooke took off in a speedy crawl toward a box that hadn't been opened yet. "You're not impressed with my hairdressing skills, are you?" Addy got up and went after the baby. She swung Brooke up as the little girl tried to push the box on the carpet. "Cardboard boxes are not play toys unless you're a cat or old enough to make a space-ship out of it. Let's go see what Uncle Troy has in the refrigerator."

She met Troy on his way back upstairs. "I'm going to get her dinner."

"I cleaned out the fridge. I have a shopping cart program. We can order whatever you need for her and whatever you'd like on hand."

Addy moved Brooke to her other hip. "Can I ask a question?"

"Sure." Troy stopped and smiled at her.

"You don't spend much time at this house, do you?"

Troy crossed his arms and looked at her. "Why do you ask?"

"Well, when I was here earlier, there was nothing in the fridge past a week old except maybe some takeout containers. No condiments other than what comes with takeout. The baby had fresh food, but everything else was ordered in. No eggs, no milk, no ketchup. You have a coffee maker but no coffee grounds or creamer that I saw."

Troy cocked his head, "You didn't open the fridge."

"No, but you did when you got her water."

"You noticed all that from when we were in the kitchen today?"

"I was a trained and qualified FBI agent, remember?"

"Ha, yeah. Well, this is one of my homes. My work for Guardian takes me out of the country regularly. So I have a house here, an apartment in France, Japan, and a couple of other places."

Addy nodded and started down the stairs. "Do you deploy with your team?"

She could hear Troy coming down the stairs after her. "I don't work with a team."

Addy didn't stop because Brooke was starting to get fussy. Once they entered the kitchen, she put the baby down in the highchair and gave her a cracker that had been individually wrapped and obviously from a takeout bag. She opened the fridge and shook her head. "Has she been living off rotisserie chicken?"

"She likes it." Troy sounded a bit defensive.

Addy gave him a quick look. "I'm not judging. Sorry if it sounded like that." She pulled out the chicken and continued to root around in the fridge for something to feed Brooke. "Would you cut that up for her?" She heard Troy doing as she asked. "I'll put an order in tonight." There were the basics that they absolutely needed, like a variety of fruits, veggies, and proteins, so Brooke got the right nutrition.

"Thanks," Troy said from behind her. Brooke gurgled and pounded on the highchair table. "Here you go, princess."

Addy smiled as she put together the rest of Brooke's meal and filled her sippy cup full of water. "If Malice and Ice aren't part of your team, do they do the same thing as you?" She used the smallest spoon she could find to feed Brooke.

"We tried that, but she seemed to like picking up her own food." Troy went to the fridge and pulled out a beer. "This is my reward for making it until I hired some help." He popped the top and took a drink. "It was touch and go at first. I'm pretty sure I had several heart attacks and lost five or six of my nine lives."

Addy chuckled, noting the deliberate change of subject. Okay, she'd flow with it. "I can imagine."

"I like the Pebbles look you're rocking with Brooke's hair thingy."

Addy screwed up her face. "The what?"

"Oh, man, come on. You never watched that cartoon growing up? The dinosaur dog and foot peddled car?" He sat down at the table.

"I vaguely remember it. I've never been much on television, even when I was a kid. I'd rather be out playing."

Troy chuckled. "Growing up where the snow was measured in feet, not inches, I watched a lot of television during the winter." His phone rang, and he pulled it out of his pocket. "Hello?"

She glanced at him, and he rolled his eyes. "No, *Ms.* Harper, tomorrow isn't good for me. Monday, I'm free all day, and Brooke's nanny will be here also."

Addy glanced at her employer. Damn, he looked tired. He had dark circles under his eyes, and his hair looked about as wild as Brooke's before Addy corralled it. She helped Brooke eat, guiding the spoon and making sure the chicken didn't end up on the floor. When she glanced back at Troy, his eyes were closed, and his jaw was clenched. She couldn't hear the woman on the other end but imagined her to be a cranky old biddy. Addy allowed herself the unguarded moment to study Troy Masters. He was well over six feet tall. Addy would place him about six feet four inches. He was also stacked, racked, and jacked, as they said at the training facility where she used to work out. The man had a body most men wanted and could never obtain. She slid another glance in his direction. Lord, he was a beautiful man. Exactly the kind of guy she was attracted to, and from the interaction she had with his friends, he was a decent guy. Another tick on her box of must-haves for a significant other.

Whoa again. Back up, girlfriend. No hearts, flowers, or chocolates with the employer. She smiled to herself. Of course, his friends were equally as jacked, just in varying sizes, but they didn't do it for her the way the man in front of her did. *Sheesh, he was sizzling hot.* Troy didn't appear to have an ounce of body fat, which she discerned by how prominent his veins were under his skin. His complexion was similar to Brooke's, so it was obviously hereditary. Although she wouldn't hazard a guess as to what genetic lottery they'd both won. They were gorgeous, and that simple fact was enough for her. And yeah, having a good-looking boss wasn't a hardship, that was for sure.

"Yes, ma'am. Ten is perfect. Thank you. Have a nice—" Troy pulled the phone away from his face and looked at the face. "Rude bitch," he mumbled.

"Language," Addy reminded him. "Sounds like she isn't a fan." Addy chuckled as she gave Brooke another small piece of chicken.

"I'm getting better, but sometimes the thoughts need to be said. Anyway, I'm sure *Ms.* Harper and I are members of a mutual non-admiration society." Troy leaned back. "I do need to go into D.C. tomorrow and check in at work. I can pick up anything we need that isn't available with the cart service."

"I'm sure we'll be fine. But right now, it is bath time, and then this little girl needs a bottle and bed."

"Bottles. I think we have a couple more." Troy stood up.

"I saw them stacked upstairs. Any reason why they haven't made it down here and into the dishwasher?" Addy wet a paper towel to wipe Brooke's face and fingers.

"You can put that stuff in a dishwasher?" Troy seemed astonished.

Addy rolled her eyes. "Bachelors." She pulled a bottle out of the fridge.

"Hey, we managed not to break her. I get points for that, right?" Troy's voice lifted as she and Brooke walked out of the kitchen. Addy laughed and headed upstairs. The more she got to know her boss, the more she liked him and the more trouble she waded into. Sexy and funny. Exactly what a person needed for a boss. Not.

CHAPTER 7

*F*lack took his beer out to the foyer and started opening boxes. On his sixth trip to the garage, he saw Addy coming down the stairs with a box and the baby monitor. "Is she asleep?" Flack asked as he picked up the last stack of things going back.

"Yes. Out like a light. Give me time to get these bottles taken care of, and then maybe you can show me around your place?" Addy headed into the kitchen.

"I need to unload the dishwasher. I haven't done it yet," he called after her. Flack moved the collapsed boxes from the items he'd decided to keep to the recycle stack and carried the clothes and other things up to Brooke's room. He opened the door and blinked. Addy had arranged the room and put out a furry pink rug in the middle of the floor. The rocking chair that had been buried behind boxes sat in the corner, and everything seemed to be put away. How in the hell did she do that in ... Oh, crap. It was later than he realized. He sat the items neatly in the corner for Addy to put away and headed back downstairs.

"I didn't realize it was so late. What do you want for dinner? I'll call it in, then give you a tour while we wait." He had a thousand takeout menus.

"Whatever you want. I'm not fussy, and I don't have any allergies," Addy said as she cleaned the counter. "I made a list for the shopping cart." She nodded to a pad beside the refrigerator.

"Perfect." Flack placed an order from the local steak house, then took care of the grocery list showing Addy the login and password so she could access it at any time.

"Okay. I've got the monitor." Addy waved it. "Show me the Taj."

Flack laughed. "It isn't that big."

"How many bedrooms?"

"Ah, seven," Flack said. Ok, so he saw her point.

"Right. Just a mini-Taj." Addy chuckled as they headed toward the back of the house.

KRIS MICHAELS

"This is the formal dining room. Through here is the library." He opened the door, and Addy went in, eyeing the bookshelves.

"Tort law. Contracts. Penal Code." She turned and smiled at him. "Are you a lawyer?"

"Guilty," he admitted. "Although most of these were my father's. I shipped them down from my family home after my mom passed away and my sister married and moved to the D.C. area with her husband." Addy smiled and nodded but thankfully didn't push for more information about his past. That was buried along with his family. Back in the hall, he opened the laundry room door and turned on the light. "I use a laundry service, but if you want to use these."

She laughed and walked past him. "You still have the stickers on them. You've never washed your clothes?"

"Ah ..." Flack scratched his head. "I have the money, and I don't like to do laundry, so I don't."

"Well, that makes sense." Addy seemed to be trying not to laugh.

"It does to me." He agreed although he'd have to examine that thought now. "Through here is the sunroom."

He turned on the lights, and Addy gasped. "It's beautiful."

The room that ran the length of the house was lit with tiny white lights during the evening that softly illuminated the overstuffed lounge-type furniture and view of the pool, well, pool cover, in the back. He rarely came out there.

He showed her what he assumed was supposed to be the maid's quarters. A small living area, bedroom, and bathroom. "Perfect mother-in-law suite," Addy said as she looked around.

"I guess." He gestured to the door to the vault where he worked. "This is my work office. Due to the nature of my business, neither you nor Brooke can enter." A thumbprint and a sixteen-digit code were required for entry. The computers in that room were linked to Guardian, but only when he connected them from standalone status. His latest case had been deleted, and the shelves and computer were now empty, but Addy didn't need access, and he'd never grant it. He kept them walking to the end of the hall.

"It looks like I couldn't enter even if I wanted to. Is that a thumbprint scanner?"

"It is," he admitted. "There are reasons for the

security and the isolation. This is one of the things you need clearance to see."

"To see. Just the door?" Addy blinked up at him.

"Yeah, but … this is why I bought the house." He opened the door to the basement, and she followed him down the stairs. "To the right is the gym. You're more than welcome to use it anytime you want." He took her into the right half of the basement. He had free weights, squat racks, isolation machines, every conceivable cardio machine on the planet, and … "Through there are the saunas. One is dry; the other is steam."

"Yeah. I'm taking back the mini part of my statement before. This is definitely the whole Taj happening here." Addy turned to him. "The sauna after working out will help me stretch, which will help with my rehab."

"When I'm here, we can work out a schedule so you have uninterrupted gym time." He wasn't going to just dump Brooke on Addy. He would be an involved stand-in parental unit and full-time uncle. That revelation came the first night Brooke fell asleep on his shoulder. His heart grew about ten sizes when that happened. Brooke deserved nothing less than his one hundred percent effort. Which was going to be a balancing act with his job at Guardian. It would take trial and error, but he was willing to fail as many times as it took to succeed in being the man that little girl deserved.

"Thank you." Addy smiled up at him. Damn, the woman's smile was something. It morphed that professional veneer she wore like a suit. *Speaking of suits.* "You know you don't have to wear a suit, right? Whatever you want to be comfortable, but suits are not required."

She blinked at him. "I brought casual clothes. Thanks."

Flack cleared his throat. That came off as awkward on his part, didn't it? Ah, what ... oh. "Over here is my shooting range. I had to have special ventilators and fans put in and a collection vent at the berm because of the lead in the bullets, but it was worth it." He fingered in the code to the range and opened the door, turning on the lights. Addy stepped in, and the expression on her face was exactly how he felt when he saw it completed for the first time. Amazement coupled with awe. She walked up to the display of weapons he had hanging on the walls.

"I could spend a month down here." She trailed her fingers over the stock of a rifle and laughed.

"Sorry, I'm a bit in love with your range. Just saying."

"Now that's something I understand and respect." He showed her how to operate the target system, where the fans were, and in what order to start them. "You're welcome to use it anytime to keep your proficiency up."

She spoke as she turned in a three-sixty. "I'll take you up on that."

"What is that?" She pointed to a sixty-inch screen on the wall.

"Oh, let me show you." He grabbed a remote and pointed it at the screen.

Addy laughed. "That is amazing." Brooke's monitor was wired into the shooting range. They could see her sleeping in high resolution.

"There's more. When she fusses, the backlight flashes to get your attention. Hearing protection is mandatory down here, so Mal thought up the workaround."

"You know, I really like your friends."

"They're the best." Flack's phone pinged, and he pulled it out of his pocket. "Dinner has been delivered." He turned off the monitor and locked up after them before they made their way back upstairs and into the kitchen. He went to the front door and retrieved the bag. "Steak, potatoes, and salad."

"Sounds wonderful," she said as she placed paper napkins and silverware on the table.

"Would you like some wine? I only have dry red." He had some in the cooler behind the bar. He drank it occasionally. Most of the women he'd dated liked sweet Chardonnay, but it wasn't to his taste, so he didn't stock it because he never brought women there. Always anonymous hotels, and most of those dates were one and done.

"No, thanks. I'm not a big drinker, but I do enjoy a dusty merlot every now and then." She grabbed a plastic cup and filled it with filtered water. "Water?"

"Yes, please. Speaking of drinking." Flack made his way out to the foyer and picked up his warm, barely touched beer. He went back into the kitchen and poured it out into the sink before dropping the can in the recycle bin.

Addy watched him. "You didn't finish your celebration?"

Troy snorted. "The celebration is actually getting this house back into some semblance of order. Believe it or not, I do prefer order over the frat house style you saw today."

"I think your friends may have inadvertently contributed to the overwhelmed feeling caused by all the boxes of things they bought for Brooke." She plated the food instead of eating it out of the box.

Flack was secretly pleased. They might be easier to deal with than dishes, but he was over takeout containers. "Thank you," he said when she handed him a plate. "I agree, but man, they came through when I had no clue what to do."

Addy chewed her first bite of food before she spoke, "You're lucky to have them. This steak is wonderful."

"They do a good job. What can I do to make your time here easier?" He cut into his steak.

Addy chewed for a moment. "I've been going over a few things. The reason you place self-defense, weapons, and clearance requirements on your listing ... Is there a specific threat I need to worry about?"

Flack smiled and shook his head. "One of my friends built that qualification listing. My job with Guardian is classified and segmented. I'll never talk about what I do for them. Still, you may be required to travel with me, depending on the circumstances. Not all environments I travel to are as safe as we are here. You need to be able to handle yourself in a situation that a normal nanny might never encounter. Of course, those qualities may never be utilized."

"Got it. A failsafe?" She took another bite of her steak.

"Most definitely," Flack agreed. "How long do you think you'll be staying in this job?" He saw her hesitate for a moment before responding. Ahh, there was an agenda. He didn't doubt it. She was too good to be true. He stared at the woman. Her smile, personality, and vibrance were ... Well, he'd say intoxicating, but that wasn't quite right. She wasn't the type of woman who slapped you in the face with her beauty or sexuality, yet it was there. She seemed to emit a vibration that he could feel, and it attracted him in a way he'd never experienced before.

"Honestly? I'm not sure. I could have stayed with the FBI, but due to the hearing loss, I'm no longer qualified to be on my team. Field work requires a hearing level I don't have. I was hoping to apply to Dom Ops as an investigator. From what I understand, they make allowances for disabilities."

And that made sense. Damn it. He needed to keep that in mind. Addy would be a moment in time with him. No matter what type of female magic she used to cast a spell over him, she wasn't someone he should be interested in. Workplace situations and all that shit.

Flack took a drink of water. He needed some consistency for Brooke and some time to figure everything out. Maybe ... "Guardian is the best organization in the world as far as taking care of its people. Let's make a deal. You stay with me for six months with the possibility of a three-month extension. That way, I can get my feet under me and find someone to replace you, also vetted by Guardian. If you agree to that, I'll make a personal recommendation to Jared King. He runs Dom Ops."

Addy put her fork down and leaned back in her chair. She stared at him, then nodded. "Mr. Masters, you have a deal."

Troy lifted his water cup. "To our partnership."

Addy lifted her cup and touched his, her smile once again lighting up the room. "To our partnership," she echoed.

CHAPTER 8

"What are you doing here, and where is your niece?" Smoke strode into the hotel room that he was using as an office. Guardian had rented out the entire building where both Smoke and his wife Charley were working.

"Checking in." Flack flopped into the chair across from Smoke.

Smoke sat down. "Again, where's your niece?"

"I hired a nanny yesterday. A former FBI agent who came from Compass and was vetted by the company. She's pretty fantastic."

Smoke's eyebrows lifted toward the ceiling. "We put a job description in for a nanny through Rio North's company?"

"We? No. I think that was a joint effort between Aspen and Val." Flack had no idea who they spoke with to get it done, but he was fucking over the moon that they had.

"All right. Are things with social services under control?" Smoke leaned forward.

"Yes and no. Mrs. Pruitt had to turn over the case because Brooke was permanently placed. The caseworker I drew is a total bitch. She showed up and wanted to do an inspection. Needless to say, the house was a disaster. I made her leave and call to set up an appointment. She'll be back Monday at ten."

"Do you need help getting the house in order?" Smoke asked, reaching for his phone.

"No, Addy and I will be able to get things straight."

"Addy. Is that the name of this nanny?"

"Addison Wilson."

Smoke unlocked his phone and made a verbal note of her name. "Going to do a quick background on her."

"Thanks, but pretty sure Compass already checked her out."

"She's taking care of one of ours." Smoke shrugged. "Can't be too careful."

"Agreed. Anyway, I'll be available for work. Addy has agreed to stay six months, with the possibility of a three-month extension so I can find a full-time nanny."

Smoke frowned. "Why only six to nine months?"

"She's driven and loved what she did. She was the team lead for an FBI tactical unit and suffered hearing loss and a knee injury when she shielded a kid during a situation. She wants to be in the field, in particular with Dom Ops as an investigator. I can't blame her. I understand the desire to do what you're good at."

Smoke got up and shut the door, not speaking until he returned to his seat, "That leads me to another question you need to ask yourself. Do you want to take another job within Guardian's structure? Maybe work with Dom Ops? Your legal knowledge would greatly benefit the organization in that capacity. Hell, we need corporate lawyers, too. You've got a kid to worry about now."

Flack blinked at the direction the conversation had turned. "Did you ask Reaper this question when his kid was born?"

"Me? No, but Fury did, and so did Anubis. Having a family changes everything. What if you don't make it back from one of your missions? Who'll take care of Brooke then?"

Off the top of his head, he could think of at least five assassins who would belly up to the bar for that responsibility, but he got what Smoke was kicking at. "I'll make changes to my will to make sure she's provided for, but I'd also like a favor."

Smoke jerked back. "Dude, I'm not parent material."

Flack barked out a laugh. "Yeah, you really are, but that isn't what I was going to ask. I'd like someone to see what's going on at the Shankles' house. Why did they want Brooke only to treat her like they did? If I do it, I'll overstep about fifteen or twenty boundaries. I'm emotionally involved, and I might miss something."

"I can do that for you. I'll ask around and see what's up," Smoke offered. "I'd say you're taking this pretty well."

"You didn't see me after I changed her the first time. If Malice and Ice weren't there, I would have driven over to Trisha's in-laws and done what I do best. And no one would have ever known I was there." Flack lifted an eyebrow.

"We would have." Smoke leveled a stare at him.

"Which is why I'm here today asking you to

find out what the hell is going on." Flack winked at
Smoke. "Do I need to call Anubis, or will you
handle that?"

"I'll tell him to give you a week, so you and the
nanny can get things settled."

"Good. My only concern is medical care.
Without permanent guardianship, I can't give
Addy power of attorney for any health care issues.
Hopefully, the judge can fast-track this guardianship application. From what Mrs. Pruitt told me, it
can take time to move through the wickets." He
paused, frowning. "This is why I stayed away from
family law when I was practicing."

"We can push that forward on the dockets."
Smoke made another verbal note on his phone to
get with the legal department.

"Thanks. So, any work coming down the pipe
for me?"

Smoke made a face. "I'm not in the know on
that part of the business. You know that's
Archangel's responsibility. I just check in on your
baby class, so you guys don't fuck things up too
badly."

"Right. Sure," Flack drawled out the reply.
Smoke was such a freaking father figure he
checked up on them because he couldn't help

himself. He laughed when Smoke flipped him off. "Just wondering if you knew how much time I had to work out a routine with the nanny. Besides, I miss the research, it's been a hot minute." Flack stood up.

"No. I never do, and that's how the council wants it. Go home and be an uncle. If you have any problems with social services, let me know." Smoke made a waving motion with his hands toward the door.

"Thanks. I have a stop to make before I head home." Flack headed out of the hotel and drove to his storage unit. It was paid for under another name, and he'd only visited it three times since he'd moved some very personal belongings into it. The drive took two hours, and when he pulled into the parking lot, there weren't any cars. He accessed the gate and walked around to where his unit was located. One key on the ring opened the outside door; the second accessed his storage unit. He unlocked the roll-up door, entered his unit, then flicked on the light, and went straight to the box he needed.

Flack sat down on his mother's favorite rocker and opened the box, revealing five photo albums stacked inside. He pulled one out and opened the cover. Images of his mother and father stared back at him, and he ran his finger over one picture of them laughing. That was how he remembered them. Always laughing.

His father had become a founding partner of a massive law firm in New York and made a name for himself by defending the rich and the famous. Flack flipped the page and scanned the news articles his mother had clipped out featuring his father and the court cases he'd won. Flack flipped the page again and looked at the professional photograph of his father. It was still posted on the website of the business to that day. In loving memory of a founding partner.

Flack leaned back in the chair and closed his eyes.

He recalled the day he found out his father had been murdered. They were supposed to be golfing together, but his old man called off. He had to meet a potential client. A high roller, which was his father's term for a Hollywood personality.

His mom called him while he was on the golf course. She never bothered him or her husband on their weekly outings, so he immediately became concerned. Then, he couldn't understand anything she said. She was sobbing and hysterical. Finally, someone took the phone from her. "Mr. Masters, this is Detective Horace."

"What's going on? What's wrong?" He was sure something horrible had happened.

"Sir, if you could come to your parents' house?"

He was freaking out by that point. "Tell me what's going on. Is it my dad? My sister? Has something happened?"

"Yes, sir. We were called to the parking garage of your father's law firm. A secretary on her way out found him. I'm afraid he didn't make it."

"A heart attack?" Troy had to use the golf club in his hand to keep himself upright.

"No, sir," the detective said. "He was shot."

Troy opened his eyes and turned the page. The images of his family smiling and staring back at him didn't register as he remembered the events from that day forward. The constant communication with the investigating officers, the funeral. His mother's breakdown, his sister's withdrawal, and his own anger consuming him. Troy broke rules, called in favors, and found out who the suspect was. A celebrity whose claim to fame came from some reality show. The police had the bastard dead to rights. Brice Ackerman had argued with his father thirty minutes earlier when his dad refused to represent him in a sexual assault case. Ackerman had threatened his father and had to be escorted out of the office.

Flack sighed. Since his dad refused to represent the bastard, Ackerman was guilty of whatever crime he wanted his dad to represent him for in a big way. Ackerman owned a weapon of the same caliber as the one that killed his father. Ackerman claimed it had been stolen years ago, and he'd forgotten to file a police report. Fucker was lying out of his ass. They had film of Ackerman leaving the parking garage area twenty minutes later. Ackerman went to trial. Twice. A mistrial both times deterred the District Attorney, and he declined to try the man a third time.

That was when Flack went into action. No one was capable of committing the perfect murder. Evidence always remained. That was what he'd been taught; that was what he used to believe. Not any longer. Five months later, while he was allegedly in upstate New York, Troy slipped into Brice Ackerman's New York apartment. Troy had planned that night since the first mistrial, and he hadn't made a single mistake. It was the perfect murder.

The cops were at his apartment two hours

after he'd made it home. He had no alibi other than the cops waking him up on a Sunday morning. But he didn't need one. There was no physical evidence. He'd made sure to wear lifts in his shoes, making any film of him taller than he was. Not that there was any video. His skill set was new and built on revenge, but he'd left no evidence. He wouldn't be caught. Or so he thought.

"Smoke said you'd taken on your sister's baby."

Flack looked up and smiled. "You show up in the strangest places." He stood up and walked over to Demos, pulling the man into a tight hug. "I thought you were retired."

"I am, but I keep an eye on my kids. Was heading down to your house when Smoke called."

"How did you find me?" Flack motioned toward the chair, and Demos took a seat.

"Where did you go when you did your first job for us?"

Flack smiled. "Here."

"And when your sister died?" Demos asked again.

"Here," Flack acknowledged. "So, you're telling me I'm a creature of habit?"

"Humans are. You know that. It's how we can

do what we do." Demos pushed the rocker into motion. "You'll do well by your niece."

Flack looked up from the spot on the ground where he was staring. "I want to. She's ... Man, she depends on me for everything. I hired a good nanny, but I don't want her to be raised by a stranger, you know."

"Yeah. I know, kid. Those grandparents of hers ... I've had someone watching. The old woman is losing it. Rather quickly, too. Dementia is what my source is telling me. The old man, he's trying his damnedest, but she needs to be institutionalized."

"Why the fuck did they say they wanted to take Brooke, then?" Flack couldn't believe the audacity of some people.

Demos stretched out his long legs and leaned forward. "Flack, in my day, that's what people did. If you had family in need, you took them in. You gave them the money. You did what was needed. You didn't step up to the plate to take that girl, so they did. I don't think there was any malice intended."

Flack slid down the wall of the storage unit. His ass met the concrete, and he blinked up at Demos. "So it's my fault."

"Hell, no, son. Quit trying to own shit that isn't

yours. They were just trying to do what they thought was best. So were you. The course of things changed. It happens. Just like when I found you." Demos leaned back in the chair. "You thought you were all that and a bag of chips."

Flack chuffed a laugh. "I was."

"You were good, but I found out how you did it. Smoke and mirrors." Demos chuckled. "You about shit your britches when I laid out your every move in your nice leather and oak office."

Flack nodded. It had definitely been a day he would never forget. "I don't regret making that decision or any I've made since that day."

"Because you're working on the right side of the law now. That first time was justifiable, but still a crime."

"Which was slowly killing me," he acknowledged.

"And it was the reason I approached you. You were redeemable." Demos stood. "That baby needs a full-time parent. Maybe it's time you become that lawyer you started out as." He walked over and extended a hand down to Flack. Flack clasped the man's hand and was hauled to his feet with a strong tug. The man might be gray and long in the tooth, but he was still fit and could probably kick some serious ass.

"Smoke said the same thing. I'm not sure I can go back to being a lawyer." Flack picked up a single photo album and stepped out of the storage unit with Demos. He rolled down the door and locked it. "How did you get in the building?"

Demos made a sound of disgust. "Like I can't pick a lock?"

"True." Flack laughed. "Are you going to come down and meet Brooke?"

Demos shook his head. "I was coming to have this talk with you. That little girl doesn't need to know men like me exist. I'm around if you need me. You know how to contact me."

"I do." He stopped outside. "Thank you. For everything."

Demos nodded. "You're damn good at what you do, Flack. But no one's perfect. You all know that one day you might not come home. Not telling you to stop, not telling you to continue. Use that over-sized brain of yours and think hard about what you want for that little girl."

Flack smiled. "I will. Take care of yourself, old man."

Demos snorted and turned, walking in the

opposite direction from the way Flack had to go. "This old man can still kick your ass."

"I don't doubt that for a minute." Flack chuckled and headed over to his car with his photo album.

CHAPTER 9

*A*ddy sat on the floor of the sunroom with Brooke. They'd had a great day. While Brooke napped, Addy finished unpacking her clothes and arranging the little girl's room. She also put away all the groceries she'd ordered and washed three loads of laundry. Two were for Brooke and one for Troy. She folded them and placed his clothes outside his bedroom door since she didn't want to violate his privacy by going into his bedroom without his permission.

She'd put Brooke in an adorable dress with matching panties to cover her diaper. Last night, Addy had washed her hair, so this morning, she'd dampened it and worked the curls around her fingers to make ringlets. She would give her right pinky finger for naturally curly hair like Brooke's, but God had different ideas for her.

"Addy?" Troy's voice echoed through the house.

"In the sunroom." She called back as she got off the floor. Addy brushed off and adjusted her t-shirt and jeans while Brooke continued to play with a small push-toy that made noise when she moved it. She'd plopped on her diaper-padded butt a few times but was more than happy to stand back up and try again. She was a happy baby and a joy to watch. Troy strode in and stopped short, looking shocked.

"What?" She turned and looked past her, then down at Brooke.

"Nothing, I just … you look different today. More relaxed." He seemed flustered for some reason. "I went out to get this. It's a photo album of my sister. I figured Brooke would want to know about her mom someday."

Addy reached for the book. "Oh my God, what a kind, considerate thing to do. I can make copies of some of them and put them in Brooke's room, too."

"Something smells fantastic." Troy sniffed the air.

"Ham, scalloped potatoes, roasted carrots, and broccoli. It'll be ready in twenty minutes if you want to have a drink before we eat."

He frowned at her. "You made food for me, too?"

Addy picked up Brooke and laughed. "Well, yeah, I'm not fixing dinner for us and telling you to get takeout."

"But I'm not paying you to do that." Troy followed after her.

"Sure, you are." Addy turned back and caught Troy looking at her ass. Or, at least, she thought he was, although he didn't appear upset about being busted.

"Well, thank you." He clapped his hands and extended his arms to Brooke, who toddled toward him. His hand was right there when she started to teeter more than toddle. "Whoops, I got you. There you go." He picked her up and kissed her cheek before looking at Addy. "I'll spell you for a bit."

"Perfect. I'll call you when dinner is on the table." She heard Brooke laugh as Troy blew raspberries on her cheek. Smiling, she looked back into the room she'd just left. Whether or not he knew it, Troy was so good with that little girl. He had doubts and wasn't very sure about a lot of things dealing with Brooke, but one thing was for sure, the love he had for Brooke would make everything else easier. She walked through the dining room and twisted to see her butt, making sure there wasn't anything amiss, like a glob of avocado or perhaps a ripped seam. Nope. She shrugged off the notion. Troy probably went for the tall leggy type anyway. Not that she was exactly short. At five feet six inches tall, she was pretty average. She was toned because of all her training, but her knee injury had stalled that for a long time. Hopefully, the gym schedule Troy had talked about could happen sooner rather than later.

"You did laundry?" Addy closed her eyes and smiled at the yelled words from the top of the stairs.

She walked out to the foyer and looked up at him. "Yes, I did."

"I'm not paying you for that," he said exasperatedly.

She chuckled. "Sure, you are." She didn't quite hear what he said after that but didn't really care. She needed to stay busy, so she did what she could. Addy put dinner on the table and made a small plate for Brooke. She cut up the food and set out the baby spoon and fork she'd found while putting groceries away. Then she poured Brooke a sippy cup of whole milk. After calling Troy down for dinner, she poured them both water and grabbed a bib from the drawer she'd commandeered for them to be stored.

"That smells so good." Troy put Brooke in the highchair, and Addy slipped a bib over her head.

"You fixed her hair, too." Troy ran his fingers through the curls. "Man, what you've done in twenty-four hours. I swear you're a miracle worker."

Addy snorted. "My mom calls me hyper." Which was the truth. "I don't like to sit still. I think I would have slowly died if I had to take one of those other jobs." She made sure the food on Brooke's plate was cool enough and stuck the suction cup under the round toddler dish to the highchair. Troy served her and then himself. She ate as she fed Brooke, catching food that Brooke dropped into her hand and returning it to the dish.

The little girl smiled and said, "No."

"That's right. Dropping food is no." Addy put the food back on the highchair and waited for Brooke to do it again. Focusing on Troy, she said,

"If you aren't doing anything tomorrow, I thought we'd go room by room and figure out what we need to do to babyproof them, so when Ms. Harper shows up, we'll have that taken care of."

"Babyproof."

Addy nodded. "Cabinet locks for in here, so she can't get into them. Drawer locks, too. Electrical covers. Covers for the gas knobs on the stove. I've ordered everything for the kitchen and the downstairs, plus Brooke's and my room. I wasn't sure if she would be allowed in your room or anywhere else in the house, but it doesn't hurt to be safe rather than sorry."

Troy nodded and ate a couple of bites. "Ok, but for the short term, if we put a playpen downstairs in the gym, she could be down there with either of us as we work out. When she gets older, the gym will be off-limits. I can see little fingers getting squished."

Addy nodded. "I think a cipher lock at the top of the stairs would make that area babyproof.

"I can get one installed." Troy pulled out his phone and typed something. "For the upstairs bedrooms, let's order whatever is needed to keep her safe."

"We'll need a gate at the top and the bottom of the stairs."

"A gate at the bottom?"

Yep, sooner rather than later, she'll want to climb those puppies. If a gate is there, she'll need one of us to open it and go up with her."

"Okay. I'll hire a contractor." Troy took another bite of ham.

"Why?" Addy frowned. "We can get a temporary child gate and install it. No problem."

Troy blinked at her. "How do you know all of this? Do you have children-rearing superpowers?"

She snorted, causing Brooke to laugh. "No, I have a few friends who have young kids, and I earned money through the first two years of college working as a babysitter."

Troy nodded but gave her a look like he didn't believe her. He made her laugh, and she realized she'd laughed more since she'd walked through that front door than she had in a long time. Being there, with Troy and Brooke, was good for her, mentally.

Addy continued to eat and feed Brooke, realizing she was happy and content for the first time since she'd been injured. She needed to be needed. That was what had been missing in all the time she'd been rehabbing. She'd grown used to being the one in control. Answering questions, fielding communications from higher-ups. Determining work schedules, running training scenarios, and working her team to be better and faster.

"I'll do bath time and put her down," Troy said as he pushed his empty plate away from him.

Addy smiled. "Admit it, you don't want to do the dishes.

Troy blinked innocently at her. "Who? Me?"

Addy rolled her eyes and looked at Brooke as she said, "Your uncle thinks he can charm me. It's not going to work." She plucked Brooke out of the chair. "The dishes will wait until she's done with her bath. If you'd put the leftovers in the containers in that cupboard and put them in the refrigerator, it would help. Then you can play with her while I clean the kitchen. Deal?"

She walked out of the kitchen with the baby, hearing but not understanding what he said. When she hit the stairs, he whistled. Addy turned. "When did I get storage containers?"

"Today. You needed them." She smiled at him and turned to go up the stairs.

"Did I go to the store to get them?" Flack held up a clear container and its matching lid.

"Yes, and your new Escalade drives like a dream, even if it's the size of a semi-truck." Brooke was a champ on their first outing.

"Hey?" Flack called out to her again,

She stopped and turned at the top of the stairs. "I didn't give you a credit card. How did you pay for it?"

"With money, of course." She headed to Brooke's bedroom. The containers cost twenty bucks a box, and she got three. She could afford to make the purchase.

FLACK PUT the containers on the counter. The woman was full of surprises. First was the tight, toned figure and fine ass she possessed. There was no way he would have guessed what a hot body she had under that loose *Men in Black* vibe she had going yesterday. But damn, she was a complete package. He'd been shell-shocked when he first saw her, and then she'd caught him admiring her fine ass. He'd always been an ass and leg man. Addy's tally in the "oh, hell yeah" column was adding up quickly. On top of the hotness factor that had cranked up many, many notches that day, she was cool as shit. The woman had her head screwed on straight, knew what she wanted, and was willing to work to get it. Plus, she could cook. Fuck, if she weren't his nanny, he'd be thinking of ways to get her into bed.

He finished putting the food into containers and filled the sink with hot soapy water. There was a new dish drainer thingy on the counter. He put their plates, silverware, and glasses into the dish-washer and placed the pots and pans into the sink. Inside that, he noticed a small plastic cube. He opened it and saw the nipples for the bottles lined up in it. The bottles were rinsed and on the top rack. That would have been good to have for the last two weeks. Not that he, Malice, or Ice would have used it.

Flack washed the pans, grabbed a beer from the fridge, then made his way into the library and flicked on the gas fireplace. Using the remote, he turned on the news and dropped into the leather couch.

"Here you are. Thank you for doing the dishes." Flack turned around and almost swallowed his tongue. Addy in jeans was sexy. Addison in a sports bra and tight shorts was ah-mazing. "She was so tired she went straight to sleep. I was hoping you could keep an eye on her via the monitor so I could work out?"

"Absolutely."

"Thank you."

He took the small screen from her and watched every move of that pert ass as she walked out of the library. He dropped back onto the couch and rubbed his face. Damn it. He'd hired a hot nanny. No, strike that, he'd hired a capable, deadly, FBI agent-type, hot nanny. Fuck, he foresaw a ton of cold showers in his future.

His phone vibrated, and he pulled it out of his pocket, reading the screen.

Harbinger: You surviving?

He hadn't seen H. in forever. He keyed in the reply and hit send.

Flack: Much better. Hired a nanny. A hot nanny.

Harbinger: That wasn't a job requirement, was it?

Flack snorted.

Flack: Ha. No. Nice side benefit

Harbinger: Don't piss her off or scare her away

Flack rolled his eyes.

Flack: Not stupid. She's good with Brooke

Harbinger: Then she's good for you

Flack: You still in France?

Harbinger: No. Madrid

Flack: Dude, WTF?

Harbinger: Chasing the dream. Talk soon

Flack sent a thumbs-up emoji and dropped his phone. He stared mindlessly at the television, not listening to the talking heads as they mulled over the most abysmal news they could find to push up ratings. What in the hell was Harbinger doing running all over Europe? Whatever, the guy could handle himself, but it was strange that he hadn't come back to the D.C. area like the rest of them had.

Flack watched the rest of the national news, then switched channels to a retro movie channel. There was an old Clint flick on about Clint and crew stealing gold during the Second World War. It was mindless, so he watched it, laughing at lines that shouldn't be funny but were.

He heard Addy come down the hall and turned to see her with a towel around her shoulders and a slight limp. "Thanks. I can take the monitor."

"You okay?" He motioned to her leg and only then noticed the scar on it. She was flushed and dewy, or that was what his mother said women were when they sweat. Damn it. He'd have liked to have been the one to make her breathless.

She made a face and replied, "Good. My knee

needs some work, but I'll get there. I'm heading up to shower. I'll take the monitor with me."

And then he was picturing his hot nanny in the shower. He took a swallow of his warm beer and grimaced. "Holy hell, warm beer sucks."

She chuckled. "It does, or so I'm told."

"Yeah." He sat it down on the coffee table by the monitor. "Go take your shower. I'll watch her."

"Are you sure?"

"Yep. She's sound asleep. No worries." He pretended to watch the movie.

"All right, I'll come down and get it in a half hour or so. Oh, the plug covers and other things I ordered are supposed to be delivered by noon tomorrow. We can go through the rooms and put them in place before Ms. Harper shows up on Monday."

Troy rolled his eyes. "Why did they stick me with the demon spawn from hell?"

Addy laughed. "She's probably a very nice lady."

"No. She's not." Troy shook his head adamantly.

"Well, then, let me do the talking on Monday. She might not like men."

"She doesn't like anyone," Troy grumbled and stabbed the remote with his finger.

"We'll see about that." Addy smirked. "Maybe

you were both having a bad day. I'll relieve you in a bit."

He heard her walk out of the room and heard the stutter in her step. He'd talk to her about taking it a bit easier on her rehab when she came downstairs again.

CHAPTER 10

ucking bitch. The words kept repeating in Troy's mind. He followed Addy, Brooke, and Ms. Harper around on the woman's inspection. Not only was she a demon spirit entrenched in a stick figure, but she was rude and offensive to Addy. God bless her, Addy remained pleasant and showed the woman everything she wanted to see. When Ms. Harper picked Brooke up, the baby screamed bloody murder. When he took his niece from the nasty bag of bones, Brooke stopped crying but clung to him. Yeah, that woman was evil. He'd killed people like her. Addy caught his eye on several occasions and shook her head, warning him not to engage. He was on a razor's edge.

123

"What qualifications do you have as a nanny?" Ms. Harper couldn't find a damn thing wrong with the house or Brooke, so now she was starting on Addy. Brooke wanted down so Troy put her on the floor. She crawled over to Addy.

Addy lifted her and held her as she asked, "Qualifications?" She smiled when she asked for clarification, but Troy could tell the difference in her smile. It didn't go to her eyes. It didn't light up the room. It let him know Addy was over the social worker.

"Her qualifications aren't open for your inspection, *Ms*. Harper." Troy reached for Brooke, and the baby came to him with a smile and squeal.

"No, hold up, I'd like to answer that."

He shot Addy a glance. Oh, damn, Addy was going to blow. That he wanted to see. She drew a breath, then gave Ms. Harper a laser-edged glare. "I'm qualified in pediatric CPR and Heimlich techniques. I am first responder certified in first aid and recertify annually. I have a degree in psychology, and I've spent the last fifteen years working with sociologists and psychologists who taught me the nuances of early childhood characteristics because my team hunted kidnappers, and I needed to know how a child would respond emotionally, so we knew how they would react to the situations they were placed in by criminals." Addy crossed her arms in front of her. "You see, I'm a former FBI agent. I know how to protect this little girl as no one else could. Because we both know the world is full of predators. You know the evil people who would do anything to hurt someone else?"

Addy stood up. "By the way, since we're on the topic of qualifications, what are yours, Ms. Harper? When did you start working for social services? How successful are your placements?"

"My qualifications are not up for discussion."

"But shouldn't they be?" Addy looked over at him.

"I think so," he agreed with her.

"I believe I've seen enough." The woman stood and straightened her skirt. "I'll file my report with my superiors."

"You do that. I'll have my boss call your boss. I'm sure they'd love to chat." Troy threw that little gem out there. He'd never played the Guardian card like this. But damn it, he had it in his hand, and he would use whatever he could to secure a future where Brooke was safe and happy —with him.

"And who exactly are you threatening me with?" the woman scoffed.

"I work for the CEO of Guardian Security, which is clearly stated on the paperwork I filled out. The same paperwork you should have a copy of in your folder." He opened the door for the bitch. "I'd like to say it's been a pleasure, but it hasn't been."

Ms. Harper's nose shoved itself a couple more centimeters in the air as she left, and Troy slammed the door behind her. "The f'ing beach."

"Beach?" Addy chuckled.

"You know what I meant."

"I do. I thought maybe you'd exaggerated when you said she was a vile woman."

He shook his head and bounced Brooke a bit as he followed Addy into the kitchen. "Not in the slightest."

"Well, it's over with for now. I'm sure they'll have to do a couple more inspections before you get permanent guardianship."

"Won't that be fun?" He held Brooke over his head, and she laughed, drooling on him. "Oh, man, perfect aim." He tucked her on his hip and wiped his cheek with his hand.

Addy pulled out a package of ground beef. "Spaghetti all right for dinner?"

"Sounds good. What can I do to help?" He sat Brooke on the counter, keeping her trapped with his body and arms bracketing her.

"Just visit. This sauce will simmer for the rest of the afternoon." Addy pointed to Brooke, who was yawning. "She's going to fall asleep. We kept her awake past her nap time, but if we put her down now, she won't go to bed before midnight."

"Maybe a power nap?" Troy leaned down and did his best silly voice. "A nappucchino?" Brooke smiled behind her pacifier.

Addy stopped with the beef half in the frying pan. "What the heck is that?"

"Oh, something I learned at work. Chug a cup of coffee, take a twenty-minute nap, and when you wake up, the caffeine will have kicked in. Works to keep you going when you've been up days on end."

"Huh, I'll have to remember that. Although working for the government, they frowned on us sleeping on the job."

He chuckled and sat down on the floor with Brooke, ensuring they were far enough away that anything hot wouldn't be close to them. He'd gone almost a week waiting for his opportunity to take down a target. His nappucchinos were the only thing that kept him sane and able to do what he'd been sent to do.

Brooke pulled herself up and started to walk. She held his finger for balance or maybe reassurance, and he moved in a circle, spinning on the tile floor as she walked around him. She thought it was fun, and hey, he could do it all day.

ADDY GROANED as she worked her way up the stairs after working out. You knew you'd overdone it when holding the banister on the way up the stairs wasn't an option but a requirement. Her legs trembled from the effort she'd put into the workout. But would she whine about it? No, but she seriously hoped she hadn't set back her progress. She'd been there just over a week, and the routine of working out at night after Brooke went to sleep was an unexpected aid to the rehabilitation of her knee. Well, when she didn't try to overdo it, that was.

Addy shed her clothes in the bathroom and moved into the shower as soon as the water was warm. Yes, having the gym was a boon of the job.

Not that taking care of Brooke was work. The little girl was a doll and only fussy if she was hungry or overtired. Addy had scoped out activities to take Brooke to during the day. Within a ten-mile radius, there was a petting zoo, a child's interactive center, and swimming lessons for babies her age. She needed to talk to Troy about that before she signed Brooke up. There were also mom-and-me groups that Addy could join so Brooke would interact with other children. Playing with other kids was a huge benefit for children.

She sighed and thought about her boss. Damn, the man was over-the-top sexy and so damn charming. She rolled her eyes at her schoolgirl crush. But like a wallflower with a thing for the star quarterback, she'd never say a word. It would be too embarrassing if he didn't feel the same way. God, she'd melt into the tiny cracks between the hardwoods and ooze into the ground.

Addy finished washing up but let herself stand under the hot water, hoping the aches diminished a bit. She didn't want to take advantage of Troy's nightly offer to listen for Brooke, but damn, the hot water and the force of the jets felt fabulous. She soaked up the warmth for a few minutes more before she shook herself out of her useless longing for her boss. She needed to get out.

Five minutes later, she was heading downstairs. The television was on in the library, and Troy was surfing through the channels. "Five million channels and nothing to watch," she commented as she came up behind him.

"That's the truth." He turned off the television, and the room darkened a bit, but the fire in the fireplace illuminated it with a warm yellow glow. "How's the leg?"

"Actually, the good leg is trying to cramp up. It does that when I overcompensate for the other." She sat down on the opposite end of the couch from him. "Any squeaks from the peanut gallery?" She motioned to the monitor.

"She's out."

"I put the white noise machine in her room. It works well." Addy stretched out her good leg, trying to stop the cramp threatening in her quad.

"Did you pay for that?" Troy gave her the stink eye. He didn't like her spending money on Brooke or the house.

She chuckled, "No, it was in one of the boxes your friends bought." She moved again. The deep ache of a cramp worsened. She twisted a bit and stretched her leg, but the move didn't lessen the tightening pain. "Crap." She jumped up and hissed.

"What's wrong?" Troy was beside her holding her arm.

"Cramp. *Shit. Ouch!* Cramp." Her foot curled into a claw, and the muscles in her calf and the back of her quad pulled up in a tight knot.

"Lay down." Troy controlled her burn onto the couch. "Where?"

She hissed. "Quad, calf, foot." She balled her hands into fists.

"All right, I've got you. Push into my weight." Troy slipped her sock off and pushed his chest against her foot. He applied more pressure along the top of her foot toward her as she pressed her heel against him. The stretch hurt, but damn it, he knew what he was doing because the cramp eased.

"Better." She panted as he added a bit more weight against her foot, stretching her leg a bit more. She opened her eyes, and he was right there. God, seeing him over her like that was erotic. He stared down at her.

"I'm okay." Her words were too husky because they were filled with lust. Shit. She tried to move.

"No, keep the stretch going. If you release it too soon, it'll tighten up again." His smile was sexy and wicked. "Besides, I kind of like the view from here."

Addy felt embarrassment rush up her neck and land on her cheeks. She liked the view, too, but holy hell, she felt like a deer caught in the headlights. Wanting to run for fear of being struck by something so powerful yet mesmerized by the rapidly approaching hit. "Ah …" Great, now, she was speechless.

Troy leaned a bit more, dropping just a bit closer to her. "Tell me you don't feel it?"

She couldn't and wouldn't lie. Instead, she said, "I don't. It's gone. I think the cramp is gone. Thank you." She moved, and that time, he let go of her leg.

She sat up on the couch. God, maybe thinking about him in the shower had made her mind mushy, but no … no. She cleared her throat, "I think maybe we should keep what's between us professional." She nodded to herself, agreeing with her sensibility even as her desire screamed in frustration.

"Hey." Troy was in front of her, on his knees between the couch and the coffee table. He put his hands on either side of her and stared at her. "So, you do feel the attraction?"

She cleared her throat. "Yeah, but …"

"No, no buts. Listen, we both know you'll only be here for six to nine months. How about we date during that time?"

"Who's going to watch Brooke?"

Troy smiled. "She sleeps through the night. After you work out, we can do things."

Addy swallowed hard. She wasn't sure he meant what she *thought* he meant ... "Things?"

He nodded his head while staring at her mouth. "Play board games, watch movies, talk, have a drink. Date nights here at the house. If it works out, fine. If it doesn't, you're gone in six to nine months, and any awkwardness leaves with you." He leaned in, but she didn't retreat. "Are those terms you can work with?"

"No. You're my boss. There should be boundaries." She winced as the cramp tightened again. "Ouch."

Troy moved her leg and pressed forward, alleviating the tightening of the muscle. "Should be? Maybe, but I don't like to follow conventional wisdom. You feel it, don't you? Boundaries be damned. I won't be the person who 'taps that' and runs away. You *intrigue* me. You're exciting and tempting."

"It is a bad idea." Addy relaxed her body, trying

to will the horrible cramp away and keep her wits about her. Between the cramp and Troy, she was not firing on all cylinders.

"A horrible idea. Let's do it anyway. Take a chance. Let me date you. No pressure, no demands." He smiled down at her. "Follow your heart, not your head, Addy."

"Yes." She whispered the words as he leaned in and touched his lips to hers. She gasped, inhaling his scent and tasting him as he swiped his tongue over her lips. His hand circled her neck, and a shiver ran through her entire body. My god, more chemistry sparked between her and Troy at that moment than there'd ever been between her and Pete.

Troy lifted away and stared down at her. "You're dangerous, Agent Wilson. Very dangerous."

She held his gaze. "I have a feeling you could be lethal, Mr. Masters."

The side of his mouth ticked up. "You have no idea." He stood and offered her a hand. "Perhaps we should call it a night and pick this up again tomorrow."

She took his hand and stood, her body pressed against his in the tight space between the coffee table and couch. "Yeah, I should get some sleep. Brooke will wake up early."

Troy nodded. "Probably. I'll see you in the morning."

Addy stared at him, willing her body to move. He leaned down and picked up the monitor, placing it in her hands. "Good night, Addison." He dropped a kiss on her forehead, and the next moment, he was gone.

Addy closed her eyes and filled her lungs with air. *Well, girl, what have you agreed to?* She looked around the empty library. She could have imagined the whole damn thing, but the ache in her leg where the cramped muscles had knotted proved that wrong.

Addy went upstairs and checked on Brooke through their connecting door before getting ready for bed. In bed, she tossed and turned, punching her pillow into submission. Was she a fool? Well, obviously. Troy was her employer. Her work relationship with Pete had made things difficult, and they weren't even on the same team. But then again, Troy didn't seem to be a macho, he-man ass like Pete. She settled into a comfortable position and closed her eyes. She'd talk sense into

Troy in the morning. Things had gotten a bit carried away that night.

Addy lifted her fingers to her lips and recalled the feel of his touch against hers. Or … maybe they could work things out, and she could have the best of both worlds. Addison sighed and relaxed. What would it hurt to try?

ADDY AND BROOKE were in the kitchen when Troy came downstairs the next morning. He headed straight for his niece and gave her kisses. Addy smiled as she plated scrambled eggs, toast bites, blueberries, and yogurt onto Brooke's plate. She was not expecting Troy to swing by and kiss her on the cheek before he headed to the coffee maker. "Hey, it works!"

"Imagine what happens when you plug things in." Addy turned so he wouldn't see her smile.

"What? No way. We plugged it in." Troy laughed. "Temperamental machines like this are why the corner coffee store exists."

"Well, actually, there was a problem with the on/off switch. I took it apart and fixed it. You have to be careful and push on the right side for it to make contact, but it works."

Troy cocked his head. "You know I could have bought a new one."

Addy pointed to the scrambled eggs. "Serve yourself. Toast is in the oven with the sausage. And those of us who did not have a silver spoon in our mouth when we were born learned to fix broken things. It's a survival tactic."

Troy scooped eggs onto his plate. "Have you eaten?"

She helped Brooke with a bite. "No, I'll get mine after you serve yourself."

Troy pulled another plate down from the cupboard and made a second helping. "I do know how to fix things. However, I have a theory. I believe the manufacturers bank on us just replacing what's broken."

"So, you're single-handedly saving the manu-facturing economy? Thank you for fixing me a plate." She moved the plate he gave her away from Brooke so the little girl couldn't grab it.

"You're welcome, and I do try to help where I can." Troy winked at her and took a bite of his toast. "I'm ready."

"For what?" Addy asked as she fed Brooke some more eggs.

"For the reasons why last night was a bad idea."

Addy put the baby's spoon down. "Care to elaborate?"

Troy shrugged. "I figured I'd get a speech about how dating me while working with me would be a bad idea."

"*With* you? I thought I worked for you."

He nodded. "Most definitely with, Ice said it takes a village, and that is a true statement. That little girl is my only living relative. I will be a parent-slash-uncle to her and be involved in her life. I'm trying to figure out the best way to do that. Guardian has asked me if I want a stateside position now that I'm taking custody of her."

Addy reached for her coffee cup. "Would you consider doing that?"

Troy nodded. "I've been thinking about it. It would mean I wouldn't be away from her for extended periods of time."

She sipped her coffee before she spoke. "Don't stop doing what you love. It'll come back to haunt you. You'll be unhappy, and no matter how much you try, you'll bring that home to her."

Troy looked up from his plate. "You sound like you've had this conversation before."

"I have. Except I was in your seat. My father is probably one of the most sensible men I know. He and I had several conversations after I was injured. I was looking for a position where I could be in the field, someplace that would accept me even with my hearing loss. He encouraged me to keep looking even though I couldn't find anything. If I hadn't kept going, I wouldn't have found out that Compass was taking government employees with my skill set for placement. I wouldn't have found this job. Which, by the way, I work for you. You're signing my paychecks, right?"

"I think so. We probably need to set up something deposited directly into your account, don't we?"

"That's the norm for a business, but I can deposit checks. I know where you live, and I don't think a check would bounce." She smiled at him and took another sip of her coffee.

"How's the leg?"

"Much better." She winked at him. "Thanks to you."

CHAPTER 11

$\mathcal{F}$lack picked up the soft fur blanket he'd brought from upstairs and laid it out on the floor of the sunroom. Then he turned off the lights after lighting a metric butt-load of candles. Good wine and glasses waited on the floor, and he stacked every decorative pillow he could find on the blanket. The pile was high enough to keep them propped up. It was his night to decide on the date, so they would be stargazing. Last night, Addy had challenged him to Yahtzee, which was fun, and he laughed so hard his face hurt when she did a Yahtzee dance every time she threw the combination. The date night was a freaking brilliant idea if he did say so himself.

Addy was wickedly smart and sarcastic enough

to be funny but not insulting. She could talk about any subject, and they were of like minds about politics and religion, which he never thought would happen. They held a shared respect for the military and the people who were on the front lines at home, too. They'd spent hours talking through serious topics, differing in opinion, but being adult enough to agree to disagree. God, it was so refreshing. The women he'd made a habit of dating weren't exactly the conversational type, and having philosophical discussions about the economic impact of stimulus spending wasn't usually a topic.

Flack knew he was underfoot far too much during the day-to-day schedule they'd developed, but he wanted to be with Brooke to see what Addy and Brooke did not only in the house but when they left for the activities Brooke had scheduled. The mom and me group was interesting, and Addy made fun of him the entire ride back. He'd never had so many women staring at him in his life. He turned down offers of fruit snacks, juice pouches, and even the offer to go to a coffee shop about a mile away. Seven lonely women who were a bit desperate for adult companionship made him uncomfortable. Hell, uncomfortable wasn't even close to the word he'd use. Needless to say, he'd leave that outing to Addy and Brooke from now on.

He uncorked the wine to allow it to breathe and stared out to the snow-covered lawn. He was falling down a slope that was more slippery than the snow that blanketed the state. Addy was vibrant, engaging, dynamic, and sexy as fuck. She was her own person and didn't seem to care about his money, which, again, was refreshing. She was mature and beautiful, a combination that smacked him upside the head like an unexpected right hook from a prize fighter. He was loopy with anticipation, and that was another first for him.

"Oh, this is beautiful." Addy stood in the doorway and looked absolutely edible. Yoga pants and an off-the-shoulder t-shirt were now his favorite outfit, bar none.

"You're beautiful." He made his way over to her and cupped her chin in his hands. "Absolutely beautiful." He dropped for a kiss and once again felt that familiar electric shockwave course through his blood. God, if a kiss could spark his body like that, he would be totally lost if they ever made love.

He forced himself to pull away. The determination to "date" her and not jump into bed before she was sure of him was waning, but he managed to keep from crossing the line. "I've opened a bottle of Merlot. I thought we could look up at the stars and visit."

She walked with him to the faux fur blanket and pillows and knelt on the fur, running her fingers over the luxurious pelt. "Is this real?"

"No. A very good fake. I'm not into butchering animals for their pelts. I mean, I could see it if I was eating the animal, and it would go to waste, but just killing for their fur? No, not a fan."

She seemed to relax a bit. "Good to know. I'm not a fan of that either." She ran her hand over the fur. "This is so soft."

He handed her a stemless glass that contained a small splash of wine. He wasn't planning on either of them getting drunk. She sat down and leaned on a pile of pillows, supporting herself with her elbow. He mimicked her position and raised his glass. "To dates."

She smiled and touched the rim of his glass with hers. "To dates with each other."

They took a sip. "I overheard your conversation on the phone today. Sorry." He watched as she rolled her eyes.

KRIS MICHAELS

"Pete is not taking no for an answer." She snorted.

"I gathered that. I can handle the situation for you if you'd like." He'd rather go caveman and beat the shit out of the man, but hey, he didn't really define *how* he'd handle the situation, did he? That made him a little happier to be having the conversation.

Addy shook her head and smiled at him. "I dialed a friend of ours in the Agency and called in a favor. I won't be hearing from Pete again."

Troy blinked as images of a Code Red flashed through his mind. No, she wouldn't … "Ah …Who … I mean … what kind of favor?"

Addy laughed and sat up, taking another sip of her wine. She sat the cup down, then took his from him. Pushing him onto his back, she rested above him, supported by her arm. "I took out a hit on him."

Troy blinked and then laughed hard. Addy was so full of shit. Her laughter mixed with his. He did a half sit-up and kissed her before dropping back into the pillows. Then he lifted his arm and rested it behind his head. "No, really. Who did you call?"

"The supervisory agent over his section. She's a friend, and I asked her to ensure Pete knew his advances were not appreciated, and that if they continued, she'd have to take action on the complaint I filed. If there's one thing Pete would never jeopardize, it's his career. It's the most important thing in his world."

"Well, then, he was or is an idiot." Troy reached up and cupped the back of her neck, urging her down to his lips. "Work has its place, but it's never more important than something like this." He split her lips with his tongue and tasted the dry Merlot mixed with the sensuous flavor unique to the woman above him.

He allowed himself the latitude to cup her breast and feel the swell through the thin t-shirt material. He stroked his thumb over her nipple and captured her excited gasp as they kissed. She slid her free hand over his chest and then dipped lower. "God, yes." He stroked her nipple again. Addy arched and pushed against his hand but then drew away sharply before she stilled.

Troy was immediately alert and ready to roll for his weapon. "What? What's wrong?" Troy heard it then. Brooke was awake.

"I saw her move on the monitor. Maybe she'll settle herself." Addy's eyes flashed to the monitor next to the fur blanket.

Brooke rolled onto her stomach, rocked to her knees, and began crying in earnest. Addy was up and heading toward the front of the house and the stairs. "I'll try to settle her. You did it last night." The words drifted back toward him.

Troy dropped his head and patted around for the monitor. He saw Addy open the bedroom door and heard her quiet words. "Oh, you are drenched and stinky. Goodness, poor sweetie." Addy picked up Brooke and looked toward the monitor. "This will not be a quick fix."

Troy dropped the monitor on his chest. "Brooke, my little princess. We need to have a talk." He chuckled and shook his head. He knew from experience that changing the crib sheets, changing the baby, getting her clean, and resettling her was a date-ending event for sure.

He sat up and looked at the candles. Well, hell. "Better luck next time, bud." He got up and put the cork in the wine bottle before blowing out the candles. Maybe it was for the best. Always leave them wanting more. That was a saying, wasn't it? A stupid fucking saying if you asked him.

CHAPTER 12

lack's phone vibrated, and he worked it out of his pocket, answering it while still spinning around on the floor. Brooke was once again walking around him in the kitchen while Addy was cooking. The little girl was getting pretty good at walking without falling. He saw Smoke's number and laughed when he answered the phone, "What's up?"

"We need you to come in." Smoke's usual humor was absent, meaning Flack had been tapped for a job. He glanced up at Addy. "I'll head in now."

The line went dead, and he grabbed Brooke. "Work?" Addy put her spatula in the spoon rest beside the stovetop.

"Yes. I need to go. Now." He handed the baby to Addy.

"Will you be back?" Addy settled Brooke on her hip.

"I don't know. I'll call as soon as I know what's going on." He rubbed his face. "This wasn't supposed to happen until I could get you a medical power of attorney for her."

"We'll manage no matter what needs to be done. Be safe. You have two people who want you to come home." She toed up and kissed him on the cheek. Flack pulled them both into a hug. "I'll call as soon as I can." He shot upstairs, grabbed his keys, put on shoes, and headed to the Ferrari.

FLACK SHOWED his identification and was granted access to the floor where Smoke had his office. He headed straight for it.

"Flack. Down here." Smoke called him, and he pivoted, making his way to the door where Smoke stood. He stopped short when he saw the people in the room. "This room is soundproof and shielded. You know Archangel. This is Franklin Harold, the Director of the CIA, and with that,

I'm out of here." Smoke shut the door behind Flack.

"Have a seat." Archangel nodded to a seat on his right, directly across from the Director. "Flack, your records indicate you speak Piraha."

Flack blinked his surprise. "Yes, sir. Not fluently, but I have a very basic understanding of the language." His mother had spent three years with the Piraha people who lived along the Maici River, a tributary that ran into the Rio Negro, which fed the Amazon River. She'd learned the language as she studied the flora and fauna of the area.

"How do you know how to speak an almost dead language?" The director snapped the question. Flack turned his attention to the stressed man across from him.

"My mother was taught by the women of a village where she lived for three years. She was working to find natural plants that could be used in modern medicine. The rainforest is, or should I say was, abundant with still unidentified plants with medicinal qualities."

"Can you tell me what this says?" The director pulled out his phone and pushed play.

Flack listened closely to the words, which were

distorted as if the device recording them was in a pocket. "Play it again, please?"

The director hit the button again. Flack motioned with his finger to play it again, and the director obliged. "He said the man dies. Numbers don't exist in the Mura-Piraha language. The way the word *hoi* said here means something, but it's hard to understand because of the outside noise. A reduction will help me to tell if *hoi* means one or many. So, basically, translated, it means the man will die in one or many days. I can't tell which without better hearing the inflection. Then he says evil man, dark, or it could be black—the word means both— hut and house. So, the evil man lives in a dark or a black house." Flack sat back and watched the look the two powerful men at the table exchanged.

Archangel leaned forward. "This is classified at the highest level. There has been a breach of security at the CIA. Have you ever heard of a 'NOC list'?"

Flack chuffed. "Yeah, I watched that movie. It referred to a listing that revealed agents' covers in the countries where they were embedded."

Archangel stared at him. Flack glanced from his boss to the director of the CIA. His mind exploded.

No way. The dour demeanor of the faces looking back at him told him there was a way. "Fuck, it actually exists?"

"Most things in fiction are rooted in a modicum of truth. I have two men in Manaus, Brazil. One is unaccounted for. He went missing. This recording was the only thing the second agent could bring out of the damn rainforest. The villager speaking had my agent's shirt, and it was bloody. Nobody could translate what it said." The director cleared his throat. "The man we're after is one of our own. He's an operative himself, and we have reason to believe he accessed and copied the list."

"Just CIA operatives?" Flack wanted to know if his fellow shadows were in jeopardy.

"No, the CIA maintained lists on known MI6, Mossad, 610 Office, and the Federal Security Service." Archangel dropped that bomb.

Flack released a breath. Holy hell, the US, the UK, Israel, China, and Russia were involved. A viper's pit with very dangerous snakes. "All right. What do you need from me?"

Archangel slid a packet toward him. "Do you speak Portuguese?"

Flack nodded. "I do." It was his mother's native language.

The men looked at each other again. "We need you to head to Manaus and act as a translator for the CIA agent on the ground."

"You said the other agent wasn't accounted for?"

"Yes." Archangel nodded. "But for now, Guardian's involvement is assisting the CIA by translating and only when needed."

Flack would rather be in charge of the operation, but he'd play the role he was given. "I understand. I do have some concerns that I'd like to address to you offline."

"That's my cue to leave." The director stood up. "Your country will owe you an unpayable debt when our man brings that list home."

After Flack stood and shook the man's hand, the director left and shut the door behind him. "This is about your niece," Archangel said, leaning back.

"Yes, sir. I have a nanny. She's a former FBI agent, and I trust her, but I can't give her medical power of attorney without guardianship. If something were to happen while I was out of country ..."

Archangel leaned forward. "This agent, she's good?"

"Everything I've seen leads me to that conclusion." Flack trusted her, and Compass had vetted her.

"All right. Take the agent and the baby to Brazil. The only reason you're down there is to translate. It should be a cakewalk. We aren't the organization in charge of the op."

"But I don't have permanent guardianship. I can't legally take Brooke out of the country."

"I'll fix that." Archangel smiled. "I do have connections."

Flack wasn't going to dispute or question his boss's connections. "Roger that. Passports, sir? I don't think Brooke, my niece, has one."

"I can arrange that. Get home and send Smoke a picture of your niece, head and shoulders only, against a white wall. You know the drill. Does your nanny have one?"

"I'm not sure, but it was a requirement stated in the job application."

"Find out. If not, we'll provide travel documentation for her, too. We'll obtain accommodation in Manaus. You'll work from there. Make sure your nanny has Smoke's cell phone number in case something weird happens."

"Will do."

"THEN GET ready and get to the airport. And Flack, good luck."

"Thank you, sir." Flack unassed the chair and hustled out of the office. A translation job. Well, that was something new.

*A*ddy laughed at Brooke when the girl picked up some snow. Her eyes went wide, and she shook her hand, dropping the melting snow. "It's cold, isn't it?" Addy dried off Brooke's hand and held it as the little girl stomped about in the yard in the snow boots and snow suit she'd found in the array of clothes clogging her closet.

When she heard a car coming down the long road leading toward Troy's Taj—as she'd started to refer to the massive home—she positioned herself between Brooke and the driveway. Exchanging hands with Brooke, she unzipped her coat to access her weapon if needed. Addy didn't carry one inside the house. She kept the house locked and knew where Troy had stashed weapons, safely tucked away where Brooke would never be able to access them.

A familiar little black car slowed and turned into the driveway. She released the tension in her shoulders and picked up Brooke. "Uncle Troy's home." Brooke babbled something and almost flopped out of her arms, trying to get back down to the snow. She let the little girl down and held her hand, guiding her toward the garage where Troy was pulling in his car.

"Hi." Troy shoved his hands in his pockets once he'd stepped out.

"Where's your coat?" She knelt by Brooke. "See, Uncle Troy is cold. That's why we wear our coats in the winter."

"Funny. Can we talk inside? Now." He scooped up Brooke. "You're so puffy in your pink snow-suit." He spun her as they walked through the garage and hit the remote to close the door. "I'm being sent to Brazil. I'd like you and Brooke to come with me. Do you have a passport?"

"I do. Does she?" Addy took off her coat and hung it on a hook inside the small mud room just inside the house.

"She will. I need a head and shoulders picture

of her against a white wall." Troy pulled off the pink hat by grabbing the big fluffy ball attached to the top of the beanie. Brooke's hair launched in a thousand different directions, static electricity fortifying the wildness.

"Okay, so we're going to have to do something about that." Troy laughed at the little girl, who laughed back at him.

"Here, let me take her up and get her out of the snowsuit." Addy took Brooke. "How long will we be gone?"

"Unknown. We'll have accommodations, and what we don't have, we can buy."

Addy nodded as she walked through the kitchen, trying to remember what she knew about Brazil, which was next to nothing. "Rio, rainforest, beef cattle, steak," she said to herself.

Troy laughed from behind her. She spun, not knowing he was there. "Sorry, I didn't hear you. You gave me a start. That's my bad side." She touched her ear.

"Sorry." He moved to the other side. "My mother was born and raised in Brazil." He started up the stairs with her.

She blew out a breath of air, trying to align the things to do with the timeline of "now."

"I know next to nothing about the country. It's huge, right?"

"Very large. We'll probably fly into Rio, then hop to our final destination." Troy followed her into Brooke's bedroom.

"What kind of clothes do I need for Brooke? Shoot. I only have one suit with me." She spun and stopped walking. "Are jeans okay?"

"Perfectly. You'll be on vacation. I'm not sure of my schedule, but I don't think I'll be all that busy, either."

"Okay. What's the weather like so I can pack for her?" Troy took out his phone and messed with it as she took the snowsuit off Brooke.

"Hot and muggy with rainfall. January is the hottest month of the year where we're going."

"Okay. I can do this." Addy picked up Brooke and went into the little girl's bathroom. She wet Brooke's hair and managed to tame it. "Picture?" she said as she exited the bathroom.

"Here in the hall." Addy held her, positioning Brooke so her back was against the wall. Troy made a face, and the little girl smiled. He took several pictures and fiddled with his phone as she put Brooke into the playpen and spun about the room. "Suitcases?"

"I'll get you some." Troy headed toward his room.

Addy glanced over at Brooke. "You're going to be a world traveler. You know that?"

The little girl stood and grabbed the top rail. Her drooly smile was so damn cute. Addy grabbed a burp cloth and wiped Brooke's face. "Teething rings." She snapped her finger and went to the dresser. By the time Troy was back with two huge suitcases, she'd laid stacks of clothes, needed accessories, and a few toys for Brooke out on the changing table. "Diaper bag?"

Troy blinked. "What did you use the other day?"

"I used my purse. We'll need something much bigger."

"Oh." He turned around. "Would a duffle do?"

"A backpack would be better," she said as she pulled some cute lightweight outfits out of the closet.

"I have one of those. Be right back."

Addy followed him out of the room. "How long does it take to fly to Rio?"

Troy was looking at his phone. "We're going by private plane, and I can ask."

"Private plane?" Her voice squeaked at the end, but damn, she hadn't considered that possibility.

"Yep." He shoved the phone back into his jeans. "We're cleared to leave as soon as we get to the airport."

Exasperated, Addy stopped him. "But we don't have Brooke's passport?"

"It'll be in the plane when we arrive."

"How?" Addy threw her hands up. "That's impossible."

"No, that's Guardian. We may be bruised, but we're the best there is." Troy trotted down the stairs. Brooke made a fussy noise from inside her room, and Addy drifted back into the bedroom and handed her the stuffed lion she'd dropped over the side of the playpen.

"Little girl, I'm not quite sure what kind of warp-speed reality we've dropped into." She made a face at Brooke. "But I think I could get used to it." Brooke gurgled something and dropped the lion again, laughing. "Oh, is that funny?" Addy picked up the lion and put it back in the playpen. Then she took out her phone and dialed her dad's number. She wanted to break the news to him rather than her mother. Her mother would have a million questions that she couldn't answer.

"What's up, sweetie?" Her dad's rumble made her smile.

"I'm going with my employer on a trip out of the country, so I wanted to let you know that I won't be able to be reached while we're traveling."

"That was quick. Knew you said it was a possibility." She could see her dad, his eyes narrowed as he thought through what she'd just told him. "Do you need anything from me?"

"No, just keep Mom from calling? I have precious little time to pack before we leave."

"I'm going to ask this once. Are you all right?"

She laughed. "I'm fine, Daddy. I'm a big girl, remember?"

"I do. Make sure that employer of yours treats you right."

"He has, and I have no doubt he'll continue to do so. I have to go. I'll call when I can."

"Love you."

"Love you, too, Daddy." She hung up and jerked, seeing Troy at the door holding a backpack. "That's perfect."

"Who was on the phone?" he asked as he came into the room.

"My dad. I called to let my family know I'll be out of the country." She held up a hand, stopping him from asking. "I didn't tell them where we'd be going. They're used to me telling them what I can and no more."

"While you have your cell phone out, let me give you a number you can call should anything unforetold happen."

"My emergency contact?"

"Exactly."

She pulled up her contacts and programmed in the number he recited. "Got it." Addy slipped the phone back into her back pocket. "All right, you go pack. I'll work on things here. When you're ready, come back and take care of her until I get us both packed."

"Got it." Troy was out the door in a flash.

Addy picked up the stuffed lion again and gave it to Brooke. "We need to remember to bring Leo, don't we? Yes, we do!" She marched the little lion toward Brooke, softly roaring, and the baby grabbed at him before falling to her butt. Brooke laughed and then climbed to a standing position again. "That's right, doll. When life puts you on your bottom, you get right back up."

FLACK SLID the back panel of his closet open and moved the stack of bags around. He grabbed his tropical go kit out of his closet and examined the contents before adding several items, including lined summer-weight clothes and a backpack with a few things he might need, then zipped up his bag. The weapons and tools of his trade would clear customs without a problem, but he carried them in a case that he removed from a shelving unit in the back of the hidden closet. He went to his safe and collected his passports. He had seven he could use, and he thumbed through them until he found the one he'd use while in Brazil. Then he put the rest back in his safe before withdrawing several bundles of cash and credit cards that matched his cover. If Addy found out about the change of name, he'd pull the "need to know" phrase out of his pocket. Hopefully, there wouldn't be a reason to do so.

Placing the credit cards into his wallet, he left the ones with Troy Masters' name on it in the safe. Again, a need-to-know basis. His sister had no idea he lived in a mirage of aliases, but she'd been so busy with college and then with married life and trying to get pregnant that she'd never questioned what he was doing. When she started in that direction, he always rerouted the conversation. It had worked, and hopefully, Addy would catch on to the fact that he wouldn't talk about anything either. She'd let several questions slide when he'd changed the topic. She was smart. And sexy. He pushed that thought out of his mind as he checked his bag, weapons, wallet, and cash one last time. He was good to go.

Making his way back to the nursery, he heard Addy singing. He stopped at the door and watched as she worked and sang softly. Brooke was lying in the playpen playing with her feet lifted into the air. "I'm done." He lifted his go bag. "What can I do?"

"I'm almost done with her bag. Would you go downstairs and turn off the soup I was making for dinner? You'll need to run it down the disposal. I think there's room in the dishwasher. Put the pan in the bottom rack and turn it on, or there will be a terrible mess when we get back."

"On it."

"Wait. Do you have a small cooler?"

"Yes, I think so. In the garage, why?"

"Bottles for her. They're filled and on the top shelf of the fridge."

"On it." He grabbed his bag and took it downstairs, leaving it at the base of the steps. The soup

lack had a newfound respect for Addison. Brooke was not a happy camper during take-off, but Addy managed to keep the baby from going off the deep end. He'd only seen Brooke get that cranky once or twice, and it took him, Malice, and Ice to distract her from a meltdown.

"Is she asleep?" he asked as Addy came back from the aft bedroom.

"Finally." Addy flopped into the leather couch beside him. "How is there a crib on an aircraft?"

Flack shrugged. "I'm assuming some of the bigwigs travel with their families." He didn't doubt it for a second, and this aircraft was the nicest one he'd been on since working for Guardian. It had to be Archangel's personal airplane. He knew the man was married because he wore a wedding ring, but he had no other knowledge about his family, which was how he'd want it to be if he were in Archangel's shoes.

"The galley is stocked with real food." Addy leaned into him and closed her eyes. "I could get used to traveling like this."

Flack chuckled. "So could I. This is not my typical mode of travel."

"It must be important, the reason you're going to Brazil." She opened her eyes and looked up at him. "And no, I'm not asking. Just making conversation."

"I could think of other things to talk about." Flack moved and pulled Addy up his body.

"Oh, really?" She laughed. "Like what?"

"Oh, whatever pops up." The roll of her eyes before she dropped her head on his chest and started laughing was worth the corny line. "What?" He tried not to laugh as he asked the question. It didn't work.

"That was the worst line in the history of worse lines." Addy rose and kissed him. "A for effort, F for material."

"Oh, damn ... I'm crushed." He clasped his

chest, seized a bit, and played dead. Her laughter was pitch-perfect music to his ears. The woman was breaking all the stereotypes he'd thought he was into. She was an amazing person, and it felt right to hang out with her.

She dropped her head on his chest. "There's nothing we can do about your topic of choice on a plane anyway."

Without thinking, his head popped off the arm of the couch and spoke. "There's a bedroom next to Brooke's." He brushed the dark brown hair out of her eyes. "No pressure."

She stared at him, then smiled. "Lead the way."

Addy stood up, and Flack followed suit. He reached for her hand and led her back to the aft of the aircraft. He opened Brooke's door, and they peered into the room. She was out but still holding the tail of the lion Addy had brought with them. Flack shut the door and directed her into what he was positive was Guardian's CEO's bedroom. Oh, well, what the big man didn't know couldn't hurt him, right?

Flack watched as Addy moved past him, her hand trailing over the front of his jeans as she walked by. His cock kicked up in reaction. He shut the door and moved toward her. She sat on the bed, and he bent down, taking her mouth in a possessive kiss. One that was more aggressive than he'd ever let himself be with her before.

When he broke for air, the woman below him was flushed, her lips were swollen from the kiss, and her eyes were heavy with desire. "God, you're beautiful." He dropped for another kiss. Her hands went to his shirt, and she tugged at it. He got the message. Rearing up, he whipped the flannel off over his head.

Addy sat up and tugged off her sweater. Her breasts filled the white lace bra for a matter of seconds before the lace was gone, and Addy was scooting out of her jeans. Flack wasn't stupid. He shed his clothes in record time and crawled up the bed where Addy had scooted. He stared down at her as her eyes roamed his body.

"God, you're ripped." She sat up and ran a hand down his chest and then lower. Her hand circled his cock, and he dropped his head back between his shoulder blades when her hot mouth and soft tongue covered the tip of his shaft.

Fuck. There was never a bad time for a good blowjob. Addy took him to the back of her throat, and his hips jolted forward. Her mouth was fucking magical. Her tongue swirled and lapped, and she used suction in the best possible way. He grabbed her hair, steadying himself and guiding the pace. A bit slower but no less tantalizing. When he was close, he pulled her off. Her lips, puffy and swollen with the sheen of her efforts, were irresistible. He leaned down and kissed her, claiming her mouth and fucking it with his tongue. Then he moved over her and broke their kiss to work his way down Addy's body. He was possessive, more than he'd ever been with any other woman, sucking up red spots on her skin, claiming her in the most basic way.

The woman under him wasn't passive. Her hands traveled his body, exploring him as he devoured her. When he delved lower, she grabbed his hand and licked his finger, sucking on it the same way she'd sucked his cock. His hips rutted against the bed. God, she was going to kill him. She was a minx, but damn, he loved it. He didn't make it to where he was planning on going. That sweet secret would be discovered at another time. Right now, he needed … Shit. "Condoms?"

She slowly pulled his finger out of her mouth, swirling her tongue around his finger as she withdrew it. "I'm on the pill." She licked his finger and whispered, "Don't stop."

Rationally, he should have stopped and found a fucking condom. He should have protected her and himself, but there was no room in his body for any thoughts other than her, rational or otherwise. He found her core and pushed in. Her heat and the clench of her sex against him were mind-blowing. He closed his eyes and dropped his head on the pillow beside hers. He heard every gasp she made. The soft moan as he rotated his hips and the sigh as he thrust into her again. Even the noises Addy made were erotic as hell.

He lifted over her and stared down at her until she opened her eyes. He continued his pace, slow and strong. Their eyes met and held as they both moved toward climax. She bit her bottom lip and grasped his shoulders, lifting her hips to meet his body as his hips bore down and filled her. He watched her eyes lose their focus and her head arch back before her body tightened under him. Her sex pulsed around his cock as he was seated inside her, and she groaned in bliss-filled agony. Flack chased his own release and let the fireworks of his orgasm explode behind his eyelids. He caught himself on his elbows, his head beside hers on the pillow, his breath fanning her chest as he gathered air into his lungs.

Her fingers slid across his back, and he shivered under the touch, his skin raising as if he'd gotten a chill. He lifted his head and stared down at her. Sweat had darkened her hair, and a rose blush tinged her cheeks, neck, and chest. "That was really, really good." She flopped her arm out. "I think you ruined me."

He chuckled. "How so?"

"I think I orgasmed too hard. I might not be able to move off this bed." She opened one eye and smiled. "But you have my permission to ruin me every time we do this. I'd be okay with that."

He smiled and dropped down beside her. "I'll do my very best."

She turned into him and snuggled beside him. "Be sure you do."

They lay together for about fifteen minutes before she spoke again. "I'm glad we didn't second guess this—what's between us." She lifted onto her elbow. "I'm thirty-six years old, and I've been in two semi-serious relationships. I don't want to fuck this up."

"Language," he reprimanded her. She rolled her eyes and gave him a look that said more than words could. He pulled her down with him. "I'm forty this year, and I was engaged once, a lifetime ago. She was a hollow shell of a woman who left when things got too real for her. I've had a series of one-night stands since then. Nothing serious."

Addy tipped back her head. "I guess I should have asked, do I need to worry about STDs?"

He shook his head. "No, I haven't been with anyone since my last physical, and I was good to go."

"I may be a bit demanding asking this, but we're exclusive, right?" There was a tendril of doubt in her voice.

"I told you I wanted to date you. Only you. We'll see where this goes, and yes, you have my promise we'll be exclusive."

"Whew. Dodged a bullet there."

He rolled on top of her. "Care to dodge another one?"

"Already?" Addy snorted a laugh when he waggled his eyebrows up and down. "You better ruin me again." She reached up and pulled him down to her. He had every intention of doing just that.

CHAPTER 14

*A*ddy stood in the dawning light and cast her gaze around the condo Guardian had acquired for Troy to use. They'd traveled from the airport in Manaus to the condo in a private car. She and Brooke stared out the window yesterday as they passed through an older portion of the city and made their way to the condo. The driver pointed out the city markets. Stalls holding every conceivable product were housed inside massive warehouse-like structures. He also took care to point out the docks where the fish were brought to market, remarking on the short distance to the market. Addy stared in awe at the city's opera house that was built during the times of the rubber barons who'd once reigned over the rubber trade along the Amazon.

They were driven to an area that was newer. High-rise apartments and condos overlooked the river. There were parks and water features strewn along a beautifully constructed patterned walkway. She could see the Amazon River from the floor-to-ceiling windows of the penthouse where they were staying. To say it was an opulent and spacious condo was an understatement. Addy rubbed her arms. The wealth Troy, and presumably Guardian, had access to was beyond her blue-collar upbringing's comprehension.

The sun wasn't up yet, and her body was confused. She stared out the window and watched the yellow sheen of the rising sun cross the river. Huge ships moved up and down the river in a quiet trail to wherever they were going.

"Can't sleep?" She jumped at Troy's words. "Sorry. I should have approached from your other side."

"No, that's okay." She leaned back into his chest. "Still a little jet lagged, I guess. The Amazon is beautiful."

"That isn't the Amazon. That's one of the rivers

that flow into it. That is the Rio Negro, or in English, it's the Black River."

"Oh. The Amazon is bigger than this one?"

"I'll make sure you see it. Where this river and the Amazon join is a separation of the two waters before they finally mix. Two different colored waters literally flow side by side for a distance. A difference in density, temperature, and velocity causes the phenomena. In some areas along the river, you can't see the other side. The branches and off-shoots are vast, and if you're not a native of the area, you can get lost in the tangle of tributaries."

She turned and looked at him as he slipped his arms around her. "How do you know so much about this area?"

"I told you my mother was from Brazil. She spent three years with one of the indigenous people of this area, the Piraha. She learned their language while working to find botanical specimens for medical use. The Piraha live along the Maici River, not far from here. She taught my sister and me Portuguese and also Mura-Piraha, the native language of that area. That's why I'm here, to translate."

"Oh." She leaned her head on his shoulder. His

arms folded her closer, and she closed her eyes. "I'm so tired and so wide awake at the same time." She yawned and leaned into him, letting him hold her up.

He made a noise of agreement and murmured in her good ear, "Jet lag is a bitch."

"Language." She yawned again. "Brooke should be waking up soon. I need coffee."

"I'll make some."

Addy snorted. "You'll break the coffee machine."

Troy chuckled. "I didn't break it last time. It came out of the box defective."

"So you say." She made herself stand away from him and yawned again. "Coffee." She shuffled off to the kitchen and turned on the light. There was a silver espresso machine on the counter and a card with instructions tented standing on top of the machine. "Thank goodness." The instructions were from the manufacturer and printed in five different languages. English was one of them. She lifted the card, looking at the machine as she moved between each step. "Cappuccino or espresso for you? I'm doing a triple espresso." She opened a cupboard. "If I can find the coffee."

A pouch of ground coffee appeared in front of

her face. The heavens opened, and angels sang. She grabbed the pouch from him. "Good. Coffee is good."

Troy laughed and opened the door to the fridge. "I'll be waiting to hear from my contact. I'm not sure if I can show you around today. But it's better to try to stay awake so you can sleep tonight."

"Why aren't you tired?" She turned and put her hand on her hips.

"Nappucchinos. Small naps and lots of caffeine." He pulled out a loaf of bread and several containers of jam. "There's fruit and a meat and cheese selection. Continental breakfast work for you?"

She yawned again. "Perfect." She made the coffee as he set out breakfast on the dining room table. Brooke fussed from her room as the espresso machine steamed.

"I'll grab her." Troy dashed up the stairs. Addy finished the coffees, then took them to the table. She poured milk for Brooke and sat it beside her plate.

Troy was down shortly after. Brooke was still sleepy and cuddled up against him. "She was soaked." He sat down at the table, and Brooke closed her eyes, yawning.

"She's sleepy, too." Addy smiled at the sight of the two of them. They could pass as father and daughter. The thought of them becoming a family blossomed in her heart. Yes, it was too early to think that way. Yes, it was foolish, but sometimes the heart needed a bit of foolish hope. Addy glanced over at the man and child. Flack looked up at the same time, and a soft smile spread across his lips. That blossom grew into a full-fledged flower, vibrant and beautiful. A family. The idea was terrifying and enticing.

She'd just sat down, taking Brooke from him, when their quiet morning was shattered by the sound of Flack's phone ringing. He pulled his phone out of his pocket. "Yes."

The fact that he didn't give his name was interesting. Brooke reached for her plate. Addy turned Brooke around, so she faced the table, and handed her a small piece of bread after smearing a bit of jam on it. A feat that was hard to do with a squirmy baby.

"I'll be there." Troy hung up and sighed. "I've got to go." He stood up and withdrew his wallet from his jeans, plopping down a stack of what she assumed was Brazilian currency. She looked at the notes and noticed the word "reais" written on the face. "The fridge is stocked, so you should be good until I get back. I think we'll need to find a high chair." He ran his hand through his hair. "Don't go too far away from the building today. I'd like to show you around and identify the places that are safer for you and Brooke. Oh. I have a nine mil for you upstairs, along with an ankle, back, and shoulder holster. You'll have to adjust it to your frame. I'll put all of it on the top shelf of the closet. You have a concealed carry permit. I'll leave that with the gun in case you have to go out today."

Addy lifted her eyebrows. "But we're not under any kind of threat here."

Troy rolled his shoulders. "None I'm aware of, but it never hurts to be prepared." He leaned down and kissed her, then Brooke. "I'm going to grab a shower and head out."

"All right." She continued to feed Brooke as she heard Troy move around upstairs. He showered quickly and was downstairs before Brooke was done eating. He kissed both of them again. "I'll be back."

Addy watched him leave and followed him to the door locking it after him. She glanced down at Brooke. "Well, my little princess, we need to unpack, get you a bath, and then maybe we'll go down to the park. Would you like that?"

Brooke yawned and dropped her head on Addy's shoulder. Addy yawned because the baby had, and she shook herself a bit. "Yeah, honey, I know that feeling."

FLACK FLICKED the unlock button on the car keys his driver had passed him yesterday. A nondescript blue sedan's lights flashed. He made his way to the vehicle and did a three-sixty, dropped to the ground, and examined the underside of the car before getting in and starting it up. Then he pulled his phone out and glanced at the address his contact had texted him before punching it into his GPS. Once he was moving, he rolled down the windows and enjoyed the breeze before the heat of the day. The flow of air coming from his speed mitigated the humidity. He drove to the center of the city and wound his way through the congested narrow streets to a parking lot close to where his contact was waiting for him.

Flack locked the car and rolled up the sleeves of his tan and green cotton shirt to his elbows as he walked through the press of people. His keys, phone, and wallet were in his front pockets, a habit to combat pickpockets or the scene he'd cause by stopping any thief's attempt at taking his belongings.

He was there to blend in. The lilting hum of the Portuguese language his mother had taught him was everywhere, and he listened as he walked. Words that were as familiar as an old friend but long unspoken caressed his ears. He smiled to himself as he turned through a tight corridor. The café his contact had indicated was ahead on his left. There were three tables under an overhang alongside a cement wall with a rotating fan blowing air from table to table.

His contact sat facing the other direction. He knew because the man's blue and white striped shirt was what he was looking for. Flack stopped and bent down, pretending to adjust his shoe so he could take in the area and check his weapons. He shifted and fussed with the other lace as he swept the area again. The small pack on his back moved, and the knife he had suspended between his shoulder blades slid to the side. His shirt was lined so the knife wouldn't be seen, and if he were caught in a rainstorm, he wouldn't be soaked. Both his slacks and the shirt had the lining, another lesson learned from tracking one of his targets through the mountains in Chile. It would also protect him against the worst of the biting bugs in the area if the need arose.

His contact leaned back in his chair and lifted his hand, glancing at his big, flashy, gold watch. Flack mentally shook his head. *What a way to flag yourself, mate.* The people of this area were not affluent, and the gold beacon on the man's wrist screamed wealth.

He took a seat behind his contact and continued to examine the area before he went to the window of the café and ordered from the menu mounted on the wall outside the window. He paid and went to his contact's table. In Portuguese, he asked if he could sit. His CIA contact's eyes flashed with anger. "You're late," the man replied in English.

Flack sat down and stared at the asshole across from him. "English is spoken by roughly five percent of the population in this nation, less in this part of the country. Speaking in Portuguese will make you less of a target. Of course, getting rid of that watch would help, too. Do you know anything about blending in? It was the first thing I was taught when I went to work for Guardian as a translator." Flack spoke to the man in Portuguese and nodded at the gold watch.

The man looked at his watch and back at Flack. "Thanks for the warning, but I think I know how to do my job. Perry's my name." He extended his hand, and Flack shook it. He didn't give a name in return. At least Perry spoke in Portuguese.

"Where are the recordings? My company told me you needed me to decipher them. My Piraha is elementary, but I'll do my best."

Perry shook his head. "My partner is still missing. I can't get the locals to talk to me."

"Locals, as in?" Flack leaned back and smiled before Perry started to speak. A bowl of delicious-smelling fish and rice was placed before him.

The woman left, and Flack dug in. He didn't get breakfast, and he hadn't eaten on the plane. He and Addy had been busy satisfying other hungers.

"Locals as in the Pirahas." Perry leaned back in his chair. "I'm going to need you to travel out there with me."

Flack lifted his eyes from his food. That wasn't in the cards when he'd been sent, but he could see the villagers blocking out a foreigner. Hell, they may block him out, too. "I was told you had recordings. This was supposed to be an easy two-minute thing."

"The recordings are shit. You can barely make out anything." The man ran his hand through his hair. "There's too much on the line. I have to act."

"I have no idea what that means, but I'll help out if I can. When do we leave?"

"Now." The man glanced at his watch. "I have a boat waiting for us."

Flack looked down at his food. "Ten minutes. I haven't eaten, and I need to make some phone calls."

The man narrowed his eyes. "We leave now."

Flack set his spoon in the bowl and stared back at the man. "I'll forego the food. The phone calls are non-negotiable."

Perry stood up. "Make them on the way."

Flack leaned back in his chair and stared at the man. *That would be a fat-ass no, mister CIA.* The agent was giving off all the wrong vibes. His gut was launching caution flags left and right. Flack shook his head slowly. "No, I'm going to check in with my bosses and tell them what's going on. I'm a translator, not a field operative. I just got into this damn country, and I don't know a soul here. You can wait for me at the corner." He wasn't a fucking fool. It would be a cold day in hell before he left with a stranger to go into the bowels of the Amazon rainforest without making contact with Guardian first.

Perry's lip curled in a snarl, but he stood up and marched to the end of the pathway. Flack pulled out his phone and called in. For the first time in over six months, he heard words he didn't think he'd hear again. "Operator Two Seven Four. How are you tonight, Sunset Operative Eighteen?"

"Glad to have you back, and it's morning here." He glanced around, noting the absolute lack of anyone around his table.

"Ah, I'm unaware of your current location. Our operational capacity is limited, and calls are still hit-and-miss, but we're getting there. To whom do you need to be directed?"

"Archangel." He'd been directed by the big man himself to speak to no one else about the mission.

"Standby." Flack released a sigh. God, it was good to hear that woman—or AI's—voice again. Normalcy was something he would never take for granted. Not after the Siege.

"The line is secure, Archangel. Operator Two Seven Four is clear."

"Go," Archangel growled over the connection.

"My contact needs me to go to the Piraha with him to talk to the locals."

There was a pause at the other end of the line. "We were told he had recorded conversations."

"The contact said they are unintelligible. I haven't heard them." Flack glanced around him again. Perry was staring lasers through him. Flack smiled and waved at the man. Prick move? Maybe, but the guy was starting to get on his nerves. Okay … so maybe he *was* a dick.

"What's your gut telling you."

"It's throwing warning flags, but I have nothing to base it on."

"Trust your intuition. Tread with caution and turn on your phone's GPS locator."

Flack wasn't sure what was off, but something seemed to be. "I will. I'd like to bring a friend down to watch over Brooke and Addy."

"Do it. You have my authority. I don't like this change in the situation. I'll make contact with my counterpoint in the CIA, and I'm bringing in Anubis and Fury on this operation, so you'll always be able to contact someone if I can't be reached immediately. Be careful, Flack."

"Careful is my middle name, sir."

Archangel barked out a laugh. "No, it isn't. Whatever it takes."

"As long as it takes, sir." He ended the call and placed another one. It was answered on the first ring. Flack spoke before a word was said. "I need you to come to Brazil. Archangel has the address. Watch over the girls for me."

"On the way." The line went dead as soon as the words were said. His people were the best in the universe. True, they all might be assassins, but there wasn't anyone, anywhere, who had the loyalty his crew had.

Flack drew a deep breath and glanced at Perry. He looked down at his Guardian-issued phone and hit the pound four times in a row and then the zero. The action cleared all of the programmed information from the cell. There would be no way for anyone to see or track his calls or retrieve any of his texts. He didn't know what he was going into, and he'd be damned if he'd endanger Addy and Brooke or his team. He then pushed the star button and held it for a count of five. The phone vibrated twice. Guardian would now be able to track his location. He stood, shoved the phone into his pocket, and headed to where Perry was waiting.

CHAPTER 15

lack flicked his gaze toward Perry. Perhaps he was being paranoid. The man hadn't said a word to him since they boarded the boat and set sail. Flack moved away from the bow and stopped where Perry stood at the back of the boat. "Where are the tapes? I might be able to get something out of them." The guy looked at him for a second and then reached into his pocket, retrieving a small recorder. "Hey, dude, the 1960s called. They're looking for their tech."

"Funny. My cell ran out of power trying to acquire a signal. That's what we had for backup." Perry nodded to the recorder. "After the villager said what he said, no one would talk to me. The recorder didn't pick up shit. Losing cell service is guaranteed out here. You should probably turn off your phone, or your battery will die, too."

Flack had a satellite connection and wasn't worried about the battery life of his phone, but he made a show of pulling out his phone and showing the man the black face. "Already dead." It wasn't, but unless someone had the code, it was a brick. The man examined the phone and grunted. Flack moved away from Perry, keeping him and the crew members on the deck in his sight as he pushed play and held the recorder against his ear. The background noise was horrendous. He had no doubt Guardian could clean it up, and if he got the chance, he'd call and play it over the connection. He rewound the recording and played it again. The man who was talking, speaking Mura-Piraha, said four phrases he could hear. The first was the word "you." The second, the equivalent of the "go" or "went." He couldn't hear the accent on the word, so it was a fifty-fifty chance for either word. The third utterance was for large quantities, and the last phrase was in Portuguese and in a different voice. Those words weren't understandable. Flack glanced over at Perry, who was staring out at the boat's wake in the river.

He put the recorder down on a flat surface

Flack assumed was for cleaning fish and strolled over to Perry. "How well do you know your partner?"

Perry gave him a side-eyed glance. "Did you get anything off the tape?"

"A couple of words. Nothing that made sense." He watched the wake of the water with Perry.

The man turned to him. "I have to complete my mission. There's too much at stake. It's a deadly situation. Are you armed?"

Flack blinked at him and let his jaw drop open. "Dude, I'm a translator. The closest I get to hot iron is in a weight room at the gym. Do I need a gun or something?" The forty-five holstered around his ankle, the blow gun that was disassembled and stowed in the sole of his shoe with five darts, and the long-bladed knife he had between his shoulder blades would never be voluntarily disclosed to anyone.

Perry grunted. "No, just keep your ears open, and if I tell you to hit the deck, hit it."

"Right. That makes me feel better." Flack murmured the comment.

Perry turned. "Look, I need you to tell me what these people are saying, and then you can get back on this boat and get the hell out of here."

"Cool. I can do that." Flack nodded and glanced around the shores of the ever-narrowing tributary. "Sorry about your partner." He assumed the guy was toast and wanted to see what Perry would do when he mentioned the man in the past tense.

Perry grunted again. Flack assumed it was an acknowledgment, but he didn't really care, nor did he actually have feelings about that situation. What he did have was another reason to watch the CIA agent. That response was off. He had a distinct feeling Perry wasn't telling him everything. Flack took a deep breath and relaxed, examining the shoreline while recalling the briefing in D.C., which told him Perry and his partner were after a fellow CIA agent. Maybe that was weighing on the man.

As they progressed down the tributary, Flack was struck by a thought. What would his reaction be if one of his team had gone rogue? If someone he knew or thought he knew had done something like what the CIA agent had done. What would he do? Would he try to talk the man or woman out of their plans? No, he needed to remove himself from the equation because his loyalty to Guardian would guide him. He would do what he was instructed to do. But what about those who didn't have his training or didn't work for a company like Guardian? What would be the average person's response? Flack sat down in the sun and closed his eyes, resting his back against the boat's cabin.

Flack knew the exact instant when the steady thrum of the engine broke. He hadn't slept, but he let the people on the boat think he had. People tended to speak freer when they thought a person wasn't within hearing distance or was asleep. He felt them move the pack he'd brought from where it lay by his side. The insect repellent, lightweight rain poncho, protein bars, and pack of bandages with antibiotic cream and alcohol pads would be examined, but the case carrying them wouldn't, nor would the bag. The bag was placed next to him again. Flack continued to rest but not sleep.

He didn't open his eyes but listened to the boat's movement for a moment before peeking through his lashes. The sun was setting. Perry was in the same position Flack was in on the other side of the door. That hadn't changed in the last three hours. As the motor slowed even further, Perry's head jerked up. He shot a look at Flack.

"Haven't slept well," the man gruffed.

"Jet lag kicked my butt," Flack provided and yawned. The yawn was real.

"Figured. We're almost there. It's later than I thought it would be. You won't be able to go back tonight. The captain will take you back in the morning." Perry lifted off the floor at the same time Flack did.

Flack sighed and crossed his arms. "Um, dude, that wasn't in the plans. My boss okayed a short ride up the river and an attempt at deciphering a language I barely know. I'm not liking this overnight thing. *At. All.* Translator, remember? I didn't sign up for this."

"Nothing is going to happen to you at the village." Perry gave him the stink eye. "You'd think someone your size wouldn't be such a pussy."

Flack jerked his head around to look directly at Perry. "Someone my size doesn't like violence, guns and definitely doesn't like to be shot at, which falls into that violence thing I just mentioned. I sure as heck don't like to sleep anywhere but in a soft bed. One without bugs or mosquitos. This nap was the exception, not the rule."

Perry rolled his eyes and headed to the side of the boat, where he relieved himself. Flack stood up and rolled his shoulders, feeling the knife hanging between his shoulder blades. He bent down and retied his boots. His weapon and the black metal tab at his toe that kept his removable sole attached were in place. He was ready for whatever came his way, and the feeling in the pit of his gut was warning him he needed to be prepared.

ADDY SLIPPED DOWN the stairs of the luxury condo. She'd fallen asleep as soon as she put Brooke to bed, but something had jolted her from a deep sleep. As she glanced out the windows, a tendril of worry slipped past her exhausted shield of repeated positive mantras. Troy was okay. He knew what he was doing. There was a reason he'd been gone for almost … She glanced at the clock. *Way too long.*

The day had been wonderful. She'd taken Brooke out, and they'd walked along the river just in front of the building and watched the boats sailing. Brooke loved pointing at them and splashing her hands in the many fountains in front of the complex where they were staying. They both took a nap, and she'd made dinner. For all of them. Dinnertime had come and gone, but Troy hadn't returned. She checked her phone. Nothing. Addy bathed Brooke and put her down for the night.

Exhausted, they'd both fallen asleep almost immediately. But when she woke a few moments ago, Addy dressed and once again pulled the nine mil off the closet shelf and holstered it at the small of her back. She'd taken it when they'd gone outside. Now, however, she wore it for her comfort, not protection.

Addy tipped her head. Had she heard something? She shut off the water she'd been running to fill the coffee reservoir and listened, turning her good ear toward the kitchen doorway. There. A soft knock at the door.

She turned off the light in the kitchen, darkening the hall leading to the condo's doorway. After slipping the nine mil from her holster, she ghosted into the hallway. If someone was trying to see her approach, the darkness of the hallway should cloak her. The knock came again.

"Addy, it's Ice. Open up."

A heavy sinking feeling in her gut landed with a weighty thud. Although she recognized the name and the man's voice, she still looked through the peephole. It was the man she'd met at Troy's, and no one else was visible at the door or beyond. Addy opened the door, and Ice came through. Her gun was out and pointing at him. He lifted his hands. "Woman, I'm too damn tired to fight you. Flack called me down here."

"Why? What's happened?" She shut and locked the door but didn't holster her weapon. Not yet.

"Don't know. Just know he asked me to come down and watch over you and Brooke. The bosses are concerned, but they aren't evacuating you, so I'm not sure what's up. Do you have anything to eat? I'm starving." He headed down the hall and flipped on the light in the kitchen. "Nice digs."

"I can take care of Brooke and myself." She slipped her weapon back into the holster.

"Not saying you can't." Ice was moving stuff around in the fridge. "But you're going to have backup. Flack requested it, and the powers that be approved it."

"And I get no say in the situation?" She leaned against the door as he emerged with cheese, bread, and fruit.

"Nope." Ice bit into an apple. "You need to go to the market. I'll take you tomorrow."

Addy shook her head. "Or … you could go to the market, and we'll stay here."

Ice snorted. "You saw what was in Flack's fridge when you got there. Do you really want me to shop for your food?"

Well, he had a very valid point. "Stop making sense. I'm worried and tired." She plopped down in a kitchen chair. "He told me it was supposed to be a simple translation job."

Ice stopped chewing and stared at her. "That man is smarter than anyone I know. He's well trained, and he's hell on wheels. No matter what the job is, I'd bet on him every time."

She bit her bottom lip and let that sink in. "Yeah ... okay."

"Aw, man. You two are a thing, aren't you?"

Addy blinked at him. "And if we are?"

Ice held up his hands, the half-eaten apple in one. "No judgment here. I'm happy for both of you. Besides, you can kick his ass when he acts like a dick, so I'm not worried about you."

Addy made a noise of disagreement in her throat. "He isn't like that. He's one of the nicest men I've ever met."

Ice snorted and took a big bite of the apple. When he finished chewing, he grabbed a piece of cheese. "He's a dick because all lawyers are dicks. The team and I had a meeting about that topic, and we agreed. Flack was the only dissenting vote, so the motion carried. He's a dick by profession." Ice shrugged. "But he's my friend. Now, show me where I'm bunking, and you get some sleep. My body thinks it's morning, so I'll need to prowl around for a bit before I try to sleep."

Addy stood up. "Ice, he's coming back to us, isn't he?"

The man stopped and turned to her. "As I said, Addy, I'd bet on that man every time. I don't know what's going on, but if things have turned south, he's got the skill and the talent to handle it."

"Skills and talent," she said to herself. "But he doesn't work with a team." She walked to the foot of the stairs before she turned and faced Troy's friend. "What exactly does he do for Guardian, Ice? What do you do?"

Ice smiled and winked at her. "Exactly what we're told. Care to show me my room?"

CHAPTER 16

*F*lack stepped off the boat and glanced around the small clearing. There were four, no, five overhang structures, all without walls. A thin drape of netting moved in the breeze from the river. He listened to the muted whistles and hums of the Piraha language as the villagers shifted uneasily. The oldest male stared at Perry, and Flack would bet his next paycheck the older man would give anything to have a weapon available. There was no welcome in his look.

Perry pointed to the man. "That guy. Talk to that one."

"I'll try, but as a reminder, my skill in this language is rudimentary at best. I speak it and understand it at about the same level as a four-year-old.

Perry pointed to one of the older men. "Find out where my partner is and if he left anything with them." The Piraha lived in family units of up to fifty people in the dry season and were scattered and less likely to gather in such big groups during the rainy season.

Flack stood where he was, looked at Perry, and, in Piraha, told Perry he was ugly. There was a smattering of laughter from the people who'd gathered, which was what he wanted. He looked at who he suspected was the elder of the camp and spoke, "He looks for a man."

The man's eyes widened before a smile spread across his face. "No. He not wanted. You talk like a woman."

Flack chuckled. "I give by a woman." He wasn't sure how to say taught. He was sure he sounded like a preschooler, but hey, at least they were communicating. "Man?"

The man looked back at Perry. "Gone." Well, he said more than that, but that was what Flack was able to peck out of the reply. The older man's speech pattern was fast, fluid, musical, and almost impossible for him to keep up with.

Flack rubbed the back of his neck and asked, "Where?"

"Water. Gone. Man knows." The man shrugged as Flack scrambled to decipher the words and make some sense of them.

Flack turned his body away from Perry and subtly pointed at the agent. "This man?"

The man nodded, his eyes flicking back toward Perry.

"What's he saying?" Perry growled the question.

"Just a minute. I'm trying to start a rapport with the guy. Otherwise, we won't find out anything. They distrust all outsiders." He doubted he was correct in that assumption as the indigenous people had adapted. Every now and then, the male elder he spoke with added a word or two of Portuguese to the mix of the Piraha language he was speaking.

Flack turned back to the villagers. "How ..." Flack stopped and searched for the word or phonetic verbalization or tone for kill.

"This man." A woman's voice filled the silence. He glanced around, and a middle-aged woman stepped forward. "This man feed fish other men." Her slow modulation was easier to follow and sounded like his mother's words. Flack nodded, thinking as quickly as he could. If the man beside him wasn't Perry and were, in fact, the agent with the list, he would get busy and quickly.

"Ask him if anything was left here. Anything they found," Perry commanded.

Flack dropped his head, then slowly rolled it toward the man. "Dude, I'm *trying*, if you would let me talk?"

The asshole snapped his mouth shut. If Flack had been more knowledgeable of the language, he might have been better at detecting the nuances of the tone and inflection, but at least he could understand the basic flow of the language, and the message he was receiving was loud and clear.

"Water men?" He reached into his pocket, pulled out his wallet and keys, and showed them. "Leave?"

The man shook his head, but the woman said, "Cold stick."

He cocked his head. "Here?"

When the man made a sound indicating she should stop talking, she shrugged. So someone had dropped a cold stick here. Whatever the hell that was. A cane? A rifle? Probably a weapon, which was the most likely scenario. "Keep for me?" He pointed at Perry. "No him." There was a quick whistle of ascent from the man.

"What are you saying? Why did you point at me?"

Flack turned to Perry. "I'm piecing together the picture here. Basically, they said your partner is dead, and his body was put in the water. They said your partner left nothing here. But agreed to give anything they find to you. That's why I pointed to you."

Perry's skin tone flushed red, and Flack saw the agent's eyes narrow. "He *had* to put it somewhere." He pulled out his gun and pointed it at the elder. Flack jumped in front of Perry's weapon. "Hey, hey, hey! Shoot him, and this family unit will scatter to the four winds. You're upset, I get that, but these people had nothing to do with your partner's death. The guy you're looking for isn't here anymore. If you want revenge, take it on the man who killed your partner. Not these people. They're innocent, man." Flack had to keep up the charade that he knew nothing when all he wanted to do was knock the ugly bastard in front of him out cold.

The agent's hand remained steady, and Flack was sweating bullets—from the humidity, not from fear—but the agent didn't know that. The gun dropped, and fake Perry's eyes shifted from the leader of the family unit to Flack. "He didn't leave anything? Nothing for us to follow? Ask them again."

Flack turned back to the elder. "Water man cold stick. Bring me?"

The man stared at him for a moment. "You take him. Go."

Flack agreed. "Yes, go." The man stared at him and then nodded. Flack turned back to Perry. "He's sure."

The fake Perry stomped back to the boat and then pivoted. "Search the huts." He barked in Portuguese to the boat crew, and they scrambled off the boat. An old woman, older than the one who'd spoken earlier, walked up to him as the men moved inside the covered area. Flack winced at how the men tossed the meager belongings. The woman's hand slid into his, and Flack felt the item. He took it and shoved it in his chest pocket when he was sure that Perry and his crew weren't watching. He zipped the pocket a couple of minutes later when all the men were turned away from him. The old woman sat down on a branch nearby and watched as the crew and the agent finished destroying their meager possessions.

Flack crossed his arms over his chest. "Well, did that make you feel better?" Flack rolled his eyes. "Dude, seriously, what reason would they have to lie? Unless your partner left food or maybe local currency, these people have no use for anything from our world."

"Shut the fuck up," the agent yelled at him before he stalked off toward the boat. "Get your pack. You're coming with me."

"No, I'm not." Flack crossed his arms.

The agent pulled his gun and pointed it at Flack. "You're coming with me. If I run across any more of these ... *people*, you're going to talk to them, or I can drop you in the river."

Flack held his ground and cocked his head. "See, I'd have a problem with being dropped in the river."

The agent adjusted his grip on the gun. There wasn't a tremble that Flack could see as the man growled, "Then move your ass, translator."

"Yeah, no. That's not going to work for me. I don't like bugs, leeches, or snakes."

Perry, or whatever the fuck his name was,

looked gobsmacked. "Do you have a fucking death wish?"

Flack threw his hands out to his side. "Dude, I just told you I don't! That's why I don't want to go into the jungle or the rainforest or whatever title you give it. I'd rather eat that bullet here than die of malaria, a snake bite, or yellow fever, or God forbid, have leeches sucking on me." Flack feigned a shiver selling the act.

"Grab pussy boy's pack and search it again," Perry ordered one of his crew in Portuguese. Perry then grabbed Flack by the front of his collar and shoved him toward the tangle of trees and vines ahead of him.

"Again? What the hell, man?" Flack said as he regained his balance. "I'm going to report this to my bosses. We clear?"

"Like I give a flying fuck about your bosses? Move, or my bullet will be your dinner."

Flack stumbled forward but turned around. "Dude, your attitude is going to get you in trouble. It's getting dark. Can we wait to venture into the great unknown until morning? Seeing is *not* over-rated." He needed to figure out the guy's timeline or intention before he broke away from the group, contacted Guardian, and turned the tables on the asshole.

Perry grabbed him around his neck, and the business end of the forty-five was at his temple, digging through the layers of skin. "Perry, what the hell?"

"Shut your fucking mouth. I'm *not* Perry. I don't give a fuck if your brain is scattered across the ground. Those bastards stole something from me, and I will kill anyone or anything that gets in the way of me finding it. We are going back to where it started and searching for what they stole. Now, shut your mouth unless I tell you to talk."

Flack was shoved forward. "Move." The word was hissed at him. As he moved into the forest, Flack marveled at the fact his hands were free. The thunder of boots behind him told him that most, if not all, of the crew was following them into the interior of the forest area. A crew member walked beside him and handed him his backpack. He slung it on his shoulders and moved forward.

Thankfully, they weren't in the jungle. The difference between the rainforest, especially around the Rio Negro, and a jungle was vast. In that area of the rainforest, the trees developed around swampy depressions. It was dense until it wasn't. Patchy with stretches of lichen-covered rocks delineating the sandy growing area. High relative humidity and hot temperatures year-round produced scrub forests with plants and shrubs dominated by trees up to twenty feet tall. Flack walked carefully around some of the razor-leafed palms that could slice a man's skin open. A startled fission of spider monkeys evacuated the canopy above them. Flack stumbled several times, not because he couldn't see but because he needed to be seen as incompetent in the forest. He needed the rogue CIA agent and his flunkies to think he wasn't a threat.

"Get up there and lead so this city wimp doesn't start crying," the agent growled to one of his men. Flack stopped and waited. One of the crew shoved past him holding a machete, and Flack rolled his shoulders. There weren't any vines in this portion of rainforest, and the way the man gripped the thing, it was more likely a weapon. The way the man walked with it, the thing had become part of him. It was something he needed to watch.

As they moved inland, Flack was passed by another crew member. He knew there were six of them total in the forest, two in front of him, himself, and the CIA agent in the middle, and two bringing up the rear. The crew was made up of hard men. The lack of conversation and complaints about the way Perry was pushing them attested to their experience. Several times, he caught the men sizing him up. They would be a problem if he were attacked at once. His best chance of survival at that point was to slip away during the night, silently taking out those awake. Then he'd find a secure spot and contact Guardian. He glanced toward the canopy and tried to determine how much light they had left.

Addy and Brooke were never far from his thoughts. Addy would be worried. He didn't doubt that. Ice should be winging his way south. She'd be okay. She had skills, and she'd take care of Brooke. He fucking wished he didn't have to put her in the position of being alone in a foreign country, but there they were. He kept his girls in his thoughts. Getting home to them was the ultimate objective. He'd damn well make sure he did.

Flack stumbled forward for three hours before it became too dark to actually see. Perry ordered a fire to be built and picked a semi-hospitable clearing, although the trail of bullet ants up the trunk of a tree near where the fire was built pushed everyone to one side of the fire. Flack sat on a fallen trunk after ensuring there were no spiders or ants on it, and of course, he made a show of looking for them.

He opened his pack and took out one of the protein bars. One of the crew, a particularly salty-looking asshole, grabbed his pack and fished out the other bars, tossing them to the rest of the men. He snatched Flack's bar from his hand and examined the pack again before dropping it.

Perry ate a bar that was tossed to him before he leaned in a half-prone position against a sandstone outcropping. He pointed at one of the crew members. "You have watch. Wake me in two hours." Perry closed his eyes, and the four other men who tramped through the forest spoke quietly to themselves. There was an exchange of weapons. The one designated to stand guard moved away from the fire and situated himself in an overlook position. The rifle he had was checked, and then a round was locked and loaded in the chamber. The man slid his gaze over to Flack, and a sneer scarred his face. It was a dare to Flack to try to escape.

Flack sighed heavily, picked up the small pack, and pulled out his rain poncho. He made a show of finding a place away from the fire where he could rest. After about ten minutes of checking, fussing with branches, and jumping when he found a trail of bullet ants, he draped the poncho over a branch, making himself a small tent. He folded up inside it and waited.

The fire started dying. With no movement to add fuel, Flack assumed all but the lookout was asleep or close to it. The careful positioning of his tent established the fact that the lookout would have to move to see inside it, so he leaned forward and slid the metal tab at the toe of his boot. He lifted his foot, and the sole dropped, but it was still connected at the heel. He pulled out the modular blow dart pipe and soundlessly slid the metal together. The deadly darts were tipped with poison and capped with plastic tops to solidify no accidental contact. The caps also kept the poison from the air, which kept the potency highly effective. He left the other accessories, like the alcohol pad, in their compartments. He didn't have the laser sight, but he'd practiced with the blow dart for so many years that the need for a sight was negligible.

Slowly, Flack took the cap off one dart and inserted it into the tube. He used the black tube to move the drape of the rain poncho back, then leaned forward and put the tube to his lips. The overlook was exactly where Flack expected him. The distance hadn't changed. He usually went for a neck shot, but that would be too tricky. Going for the heart, he could hit the ribs, and the poison would take too long to work. The dart was almost immediate if it hit a vein. Flack lowered his gaze. The man sat on a log. His legs were open, knees wide, and the rifle was propped against one thigh.

Flack drew a huge lungful of air and targeted the apex of the man's legs, slightly to the side of center. He let the dart fly, placing another dart in the tube as soon as his current one left the gun.

The man twitched and attempted to stand but dropped to his ass. He attempted to grab the dart, to scream for help, but the poison hit his system and stopped all muscle movement. Flack glanced around at Perry. The man hadn't moved, but his lips and face were slack and relaxed. Flack maneuvered out of the small tent, leaving it as a drape to camouflage his escape, but one of the men at the fire stirred and sat up. Flack turned, aimed, and let the second dart fly. The man slumped and rolled to his side in a contorted heap. Flack waited, watching for any further movement. He wouldn't kill just to kill, and he didn't have a coded mission. Unfortunately, the lookout and second crew member were casualties of his need to escape. It sucked, but it happened sometimes. Carefully, silently, and diligently, he moved due east toward whatever location Perry was pushing them, assuming Perry would think he'd go back toward the boat. He traveled as soundlessly as possible until he was far enough away from the camp to call Guardian.

Flack backed into a low tangle of soft palms and shrubs and went to his knees. The stench of something dead and decaying hit him hard. He looked around and moved away from whatever animal had crawled under the leaves to die. Unfortunately, he'd kneeled in some juicy portion of the animal. Whatever. He would share the area with the dead thing because the leaves would filter any light that the screen of his phone would emit.

"Operative Two Seven Four. A very early good morning, Sunset Operative Eighteen."

No matter how nice it was to hear her voice again, he was in a hurry. "I need to speak to Archangel."

"He is out of reach at the moment. I've been directed to reroute you. Standby."

Flack rubbed his eyes. He was jet lagged and exhausted, but he was free. He heard yelling. The sound stirred the animals of the forest for a moment. Perry knew he was gone, and it didn't sound like he was so happy about it.

"Fury online."

"The line is secure. Operator Two Seven Four is clear."

Flack didn't spend any time on trivial shit. "The person I was told to meet is dead. So is his partner. I'm in the middle of the fucking Amazon." He was also tired, sweaty, and starving, but Fury didn't need to know that.

Fury made a huffing sound. Flack wasn't sure what it meant, but he listened as the assassin spoke, "Archangel is meeting with his counterparts now. Here is the sit rep. This is a coded and sanctioned operation. Your target is Keith Bowman. CCS is sending a picture. He's fluent in Portuguese and English. We need you to locate Bowman and obtain the list."

Flack shielded the phone with his body to eliminate as much light from the screen as possible and saw the picture of the man he'd thought was Perry. "Locating him won't be a problem. I just left him and slid into the forest. I can go back and take care of the bastard. To clarify, you said he was coded?" He unzipped his top pocket, pulled out a small plastic stick, and examined it with the light of his phone.

"Yes." Fury confirmed. "But the important thing is the list."

"Hold on a sec. Yeah, well, I believe I have that in my hand. That is if the list could be on an SD card." He traced his fingers over the tiny chip encased in the plastic sheath.

"That's exactly what it should be on, according to the CIA. Get the hell out of there and make your way back to Manaus. Flack, I cannot state this clearly enough: Bowman, nor anyone else, can get their hands on that list. Understood?"

"Understood." Flack rotated the small SD card in his fingertips. "I can destroy it now."

"If necessity dictates, do so. If not, there may be information on the card that shows what avenue Bowman took to access the data and with whom he was working. Programming or mapping shit I don't understand, but smarter people do. There was no way he was working alone." Fury's voice lowered. "If you have to destroy it, do it. No one else gets that list."

"That's a good copy. What was this fucker going to do? Release the names?" Flack listened to something moving under the root system of the tree he was near. Nothing like the sound of foot-steps that a human or a large animal would make. Probably a rat or nocturnal hunter. Maybe a snake.

"The bastard is going to sell it to the highest bidder. The auction date is one week from today. Our computer specialists are trying to locate the source of his last broadcast on the dark web. They've narrowed it down to Manaus, so that's where we'll start the hunt for the bastard once we have the list. End that bastard if you can, but the list … Damn, bring that bitch home. Destroy the list only if necessary. If anyone else gets their hands on it, the world will slide into a raging dumpster fire. We have assets relocating to monitor the entities we know will try to lay claim to it should you fail to get it out of the jungle. Don't fail."

"I'll need a boat for extract. I'm shooting for five clicks to the east of my current location. GPS is on and active. I'll be there just after sun-up." He'd rather take out Bowman and any of his crew who happened to be so unlucky to get in the way, but backtracking would mean he wouldn't make it to the rally point by that time.

"They will wait for you. Get the fuck out of there and back to civilization."

"I copy. Fury …"

"They're safe. Bring us the list. That is the priority. Bowman can wait, he's a marked man, and he's living on borrowed time. The Rose is clear." Fury knew what he was asking without him having to say it.

Flack snapped the cover back on the chip and slid it into his pocket, making sure to zip it shut. It was time to move and move quickly. He worked his way out of the clump of palms and drew a breath of fresh air before orienting himself. He turned to the east and hustled. He had a boat to catch.

CHAPTER 17

Flack stepped onto the fishing boat that the crew had tied to the shore exactly where he'd requested the evac. The Brazilian crew didn't ask any questions but did point him to a basket equipped with cool water and a sandwich the size of his head. He made quick work of both. Once they were a few miles down the river and no one was following them, Flack made another call.

"Operator Two Seven Four, standby for Archangel." Flack closed his eyes and dropped his head back on the ship's bulkhead. He loved that operator. Whoever the hell she was.

"Archangel on the line."

"Sir, the line is secure. Operator Two Seven Four is clear."

"I'm on the boat heading toward Manaus." And he was dead tired.

"Copy that. The list?"

"In my pocket." He'd only checked the damn thing every other minute during his night-time walk and early morning sprint through the forest.

"Bowman?"

"I didn't double back for him. When he doesn't find me, he'll know he was played. He'll be heading back to the city, too." Hell, the darts would tell him that, too.

"Played?" Archangel seemed to be confused.

"I told him I was a translator and acted like a pansy-ass. He assumed I didn't have the balls to venture into the forest alone. I'm pretty sure selling him on that premise was the only reason I wasn't secured to a tree last night."

"Good call, then. We don't have a secure place to analyze that chip in Brazil, so you'll have to hand-carry it. Gather your family and head to the airport. My jet is still down there from taking Ice south. You'll fly back on it as soon as you can get there."

"What about Bowman?"

"Ice will take that portion of the assignment." Archangel didn't sound like he'd be open to suggestions on the point.

"Copy that."

"I'll contact Ice and give him a sit rep. Get on that plane and don't give that chip to anyone or let it out of your possession until you personally hand it to Smoke or me. One of us will meet you at the airport."

"Understood."

"You did well, Flack."

"I'll always do what it takes, sir."

"For as long as it takes, I know. However, I'm suggesting you consider doing it from the States from now on. Your family needs you to be home, not running through the rainforests of the Amazon."

Flack chuckled. "I love the research I do for the council and the reason I do it."

"Then we'll keep you on in that capacity. There are others who can step in and handle the action portion of your particular specialty."

He opened his eyes and stared at another boat in the distance, downriver from where the boat he was traveling in had come. "You may be catching me at a weak moment, but that sounds like a compromise I'd be willing to make. I'll check in when we've boarded the plane."

"I won't hold you to the answer. Consider it. Sleep on it, and we'll talk when you get back. Do you need Ice to meet you at the harbor?"

"No, sir. Bowman shouldn't be ahead of me, and I have a car parked not far from the old ports. I'll be cautious, but I don't see any issues arising. Thank you for the offer, sir." He was more than capable of handling anything that stood between him and the girls. Permanently ending any threat wasn't an issue.

"If you have problems, you know the drill."

"Yes, sir, clear the scene and report in so you can manage the media and local authorities."

"Again, good job, Flack. Archangel is clear."

Flack disconnected and stared at the boat following them down the river. The color was off, so it wasn't Bowman. However, the three boats past that one were on his scope, too. He'd be paranoid as hell until he handed the disk in his pocket to whoever met them at the airport.

He switched his gaze to the other horizon and

watched as the city of Manaus appeared. All things considered, he knew Archangel was right about Brooke needing him home. His relationship with Addy was new, but it was … Damn it was good. She spoke his work language. She knew tactics and weapons and understood, to a degree, his current life. The chemistry between them was freaking off the charts, too. Couple that with the fact that she was amazing with Brooke, and damn, she was the complete package. He'd never been more serious about his intent on a relationship before. Hopefully, Addy was of the same mindset, but only time would tell if they were meant to be together for the long haul. At that point, anything could shake the relationship apart.

When the boat docked, he saluted the crew and made tracks back to the rented car he'd parked a little more than twenty-four hours ago. He did a cursory walk around and checked the undercarriage of the car before unlocking it and heading back to Addy and Brooke. He didn't drive straight there, however. A niggling at the base of his neck had him watching the rearview as much as the traffic in front of him. He took random turns, pulled over, and parked several times, but still, there was nothing.

Flack pulled into the parking lot of the luxury condos and waited. No cars followed him. He entered one building, walked out of the back, and hot-footed it over to his tower. He used the stairs instead of the elevator and waited, listening for any sounds of someone following him. Nothing.

He opened the door and headed to the condo Guardian had rented. At his soft knock, the door opened, and Ice gave him a smirk. "Saw you getting out of the car. Took you long enough." Ice whispered the words, and Flack continued in kind. What they would talk about didn't need to go further than the two of them. Flack slid into the hallway. "The girls?"

"Fine. Addy is up with Brooke, putting her down for a nap. Archangel called and filled me in. Do you think you were followed?" Ice backed up a step. "Man, you reek."

"Thanks, dickwad." Flack leaned back against the wall. "My gut tells me something is off. You got the package on this guy?"

"I did. Any intel you can give me?"

"He's driven but not the sharpest tack in the box. I can't help but think he's not the mastermind of this operation, so watch out."

"Yeah, and why hide out in the middle of the

Amazon? Other cities would provide better coverage and subterfuge," Ice added.

"Too many questions. I'm going to go up and grab the girls. We need to leave, like now."

"Understood. The airfield?"

"Yes."

"I figured. Make sure to send that private plane back for me. Man, that was some plush, right there."

"Like I have a say in where that thing flies." Flack chuckle. "Thank you, man. For taking care of them."

"She didn't need it. She had a nine-mil point blank in my face when I knocked in the middle of the night. She's solid. I'm glad you two are together."

"So am I," Addy said from the bottom of the stairs. Flack walked up to her and wrapped her in his arms. She hugged him and then coughed, pulling away a bit. "God, you stink."

"See? I wasn't being a dickwad." Ice chuckled. "I've got your six until you're in the air. Do everyone a favor and shower before you leave." He opened the door and walked out, closing it behind him.

Addy picked up on the terminology. "We're leaving? Now?"

"Yes. As soon as possible."

"Are we in danger?" She hustled to the stairs.

"Unknown, but there's a possibility." Simply because of the SD card he had in his pocket.

She almost ran up the carpeted stairs. "All right. Give me five minutes. Please shower. You really do smell."

He didn't doubt it. The grime that covered him and the sweat that caked the grime to him were thick enough to scratch off, and the dead animal he'd knelt in last night had to add to that aroma. But ... "No time. There's a bathroom on the plane." He'd used less to clean up. Besides, the possibility of the list in his pocket walking away at thirty-five-thousand feet was next to nil.

He moved into the bedroom and shoved the few items he'd removed into his go bag before grabbing what he could see of Addy's things and tossing them into her bag. She came into the room. "Brooke's bags are packed. I'll get the cooler with the formula."

"I'll take the bags down." Flack grabbed his, Addy's, and Brooke's bags in the same hand, leaving his right hand free in case he needed his weapon. He didn't bother deviating. Ice had his six, so he knew the man would stop anyone trying to trail or track them.

He was heading back into the building when Addy, carrying Brooke, the backpack, and the cooler, exited the building. "I locked the door on the way out and made sure everything was unplugged."

"Perfect. The blue piece of shit over there is our ride."

"Luxury at its finest, and as long as it gets us to where we're going safely, I don't care." Addy gave him the cooler and waited as he helped her take the backpack off.

Brooke squirmed a bit as Addy got her into the front seat of the car. Flack got in after he stowed the items he'd taken from Addy, then pulled out of the parking lot. He passed Ice's vehicle, and the man pulled out behind him, slowing to put some distance between them.

"Turn the air on, please. Lord, what did you step in?" Addy waved her hand in front of her face. Just then, a rumble from Brooke's diapers ripped through the car. So did the stench.

"Oh, crap." Addy sighed.

"Literally." Flack laughed.

"I'll change her as soon as we get to the airport while you're getting the bags on the plane. That way, we don't fly halfway around the world with a weapon of mass destruction. Seriously, turn the air on."

He messed with the buttons on the dash until air started to pour out the vents. Flack canvassed the front and rear views. Ice's vehicle was barely visible in Manaus' heavy midday traffic. The GPS on his phone rerouted them around two traffic accidents, but the drive slowed to a crawl. A trip that should have taken fifteen minutes took almost an hour. Needless to say, Addy changed Brooke during the drive. She grumbled about not having a car seat, but Flack could do nothing about it except drive carefully.

Finally, Flack pulled the old car in front of the private terminal and rushed to the passenger side, helping Addy and Brooke out of the car. "I'm going to change her again and make sure I got everything cleaned up. She wasn't too cooperative."

"I'll take the bags through." He gave her the backpack and grabbed the other bags from the back of the car. Addy marched in and headed straight to the bathroom. Flack stopped at the counter and was told where their plane was parked and that the crew was upstairs filing a flight plan with the local authorities. Flack thanked the woman who had the decency not to mention his smell, although she did take a step back when talking to him. He headed to the black jet in the second hangar and had just about hit the retractable steps when he heard the very distinct click of metal on metal.

He stopped in his tracks. "You have something of mine, I believe?" a voice behind him said in Portuguese.

Flack turned around with his hands still full of bags. He sat them down and lifted his arms. "I'm not sure who you think I am, but I don't know you." He answered in English as he stared at the man in front of him.

"The name is Perry."

"Ah." Flack linked his fingers and put both his hands behind his neck. He dipped his fingers down and grabbed the fine leather sling holding his throwing knife. "So, did you kill Bowman?"

"No, he's watching the front of the building. He kept out of sight until you showed up."

"How did you know I'd be coming here?"

"Unlike Bowman, I use my brain, not my brawn. It wasn't too hard to figure out. A Guardian translator mysteriously disappears from the middle of the rainforest, leaving poisonous darts in his wake. You wouldn't wait to travel, so a private plane was the logical conclusion. Your crew has been delayed, by the way. I'd like my card now, please." The man extended his hand but kept his gun trained on Flack.

"I don't have it." Flack shrugged and used the motion to pull the hilt of his knife to his fingertips. The sheath fell down his back again once he had the hilt in his grip.

Perry chuckled. "Oh, but you do. You see, that man in the village knew more than he was letting on. When I tortured him, he spoke enough Portuguese for me to understand they gave it to you." Perry's smile slid from his face. "Torture was something Bowman should have done from the beginning."

"Where is your other partner?"

"Torn apart by a group of black caimans after he decided he didn't want to proceed with the plan. Alligators aren't picky about what they eat. I'm done being kind. Give me the card. Now." Perry pulled the hammer of the automatic back, which was just for show because the damn thing would fire if he pulled the hammer back or not.

At that moment, Addy walked around the corner of the door. Perry swung in her direction, and Flack launched the knife. Because of Perry's twist, the knife embedded itself in the man's shoulder. Flack was in the process of dropping to pull his handgun when he heard the repeated pop of Addy's weapon.

Flack vaulted to the left as he grabbed his automatic. He landed on the tarmac, with his weapon pointed at Perry, who was bleeding out. Addy moved forward, her weapon trained on Perry.

Flack saw Bowman as he rounded the corner. "Down!" He screamed the word, and Addy dropped like a rock to the hangar floor. He fired three shots into Bowman's chest. The man dropped like a rock, but it wasn't just his weapon that fired. Ice rounded the corner with his weapon pulled and still trained on Bowman. Flack moved faster than he'd ever moved, scrambling to get to Addy as soon as he could. "Are you all right? Where's Brooke?"

"I'm fine. Brooke's with the receptionist in the building. Ice told me he'd seen this guy playing lookout. We figured he wasn't working alone." Addy stood up and wiped off her jeans. "They aren't going to talk."

"The one I have in my truck will," Ice said.

Flack turned to him. "American?"

"Definitely." Ice nodded.

"All right. Addy, get Brooke. Ice, the crew was supposed to be upstairs filing a flight plan. See if they made it. I'll call this in."

"Done," Ice said as Addy holstered her weapon and ran out of the hanger. Flack put his hand over the card. His weapon still clutched in the hand that covered his pocket. He sat down on the silver step and stared at the dead men. The dead men who could have taken Brooke from him if Addy and Ice hadn't thought quickly. Fuck. Archangel was right. Brooke deserved better.

He opened the phone and hit recall. "Operator Two Seven Four. Standby Sunset Operative Eighteen, I'm rerouting your call to Archangel."

Flack said nothing as he watched the pool of blood around the real Perry grow thicker and spread.

"Archangel online."

"The call is secure. Operator Two Seven Four is clear."

"Bowman and Perry are down. Ice has one alive in his vehicle. The status of the aircrew is unknown."

"Your family?"

"Safe."

"The list?"

"Secure."

"Affirmative. Location?"

"The hangar where the jet is located."

"I copy. I'll call you back."

The line went dead. Flack's head jerked up when he heard Brooke laugh. Addy had a blanket over her and Brooke's heads. "We're playing peek-a-boo. Yes, we are. I bet Uncle Troy can't find us." The little girl laughed again, and he once again thanked fortune for putting Addy in his path. Brooke wouldn't see the dead men while they played. He guided them to the plane with his voice and, at the steps, took the blanket off, playing peek-a-boo. His frame blocked Brooke's view, and Addy hustled the baby into the aircraft.

Ice, directing a man who was gagged and bound, and two crew members returned to the hangar. "Boss man says we're coming home with you," Ice said as he shoved the man in front of him up the steps.

"We'll do another preflight in case those assholes fucked with the plane," one of the pilots said.

"I thought I gave this shit up when I moved from the teams," the other grumbled.

"Suck it up, buttercup." The other one nodded at Flack. "I've got your bags."

"Thanks." Flack moved out of the way. The pilot waved his hand in front of his face. "Dude, there's a shower on board. I'd suggest using it."

Flack rolled his eyes heavenward. "Just do what you need to do. This place will be swarming with locals soon."

"Don't we know it," the pilot agreed and took the bags to the rear of the plane after Flack rescued the cooler and the backpack.

He made his way into the plane and chuckled at the blanket over the head of the man Ice had bound and gagged. He was seat belted and as far away from Addy and Brooke as humanly possible for takeoff.

Brooke reached for him, and he picked her up. "Hey, sweetie. Were you a good girl for Addy?"

It took about five seconds before she arched back and said "No" as distinctly as any word he'd ever heard. She pushed her arms against his chest.

"All right, all right." He handed her back to Addy. "I get the message. A shower is needed."

"That's what I told you," Ice said from where he

sat across from his detainee. "Does this thing have any food?"

Flack snorted and dropped into a chair far enough away from everyone to keep his stench to himself. He hoped.

CHAPTER 18

As soon as they were in the air, Addy took Brooke into the bedroom. Troy followed them. "Hey, are you okay?" He stayed in the doorway.

She shook her head. "No, not really. Right now, I should be answering questions from the local authorities."

"Any questions the locals have will all be answered. What we're doing now is so much more important than those two dead men. I wish I could tell you more, but this is beyond a top-secret clearance and in the realm where I normally operate."

Brooke yawned and leaned against her chest. Her hand tapped Addy's cheek. "You're tired, aren't you?" She glanced at Troy as she cuddled the little

237

girl and started to rock back and forth. "I'm involved in this situation to my eyeballs. I ..." she looked down at Brooke before continuing, "un-alived a man. Granted, it was justified, and I would do it again in a heartbeat. I'd like you to ask your superiors for a little leeway in filling in at least the shadows of this situation for me."

A quick smile flashed across Troy's face as if she'd said something funny. She frowned. "I didn't think she needed to hear that word."

"Un-alived wasn't what was funny, I assure you. I'm going to grab a shower. Ice is settled for the moment. Can I get you anything before I get some of this grime off me?"

"A bottle for her? She missed her nap, and I have no idea what time it will be when we land, so I'm just going to let her sleep." Addy kissed Brooke's head.

"I can do that. I'll be right back." Troy disappeared from the doorway.

She whispered to the little angel in her arms, "I'm still worried. My training tells me this isn't the way things are supposed to be."

Brooke pushed away from her and yawned hugely. "Ba-ba."

"Yep, Uncle Troy is getting your bottle. You're

such a smart girl, aren't you?" Addy hugged the baby. Troy stopped in the doorway and stretched the bottle toward Addy, and she took it and popped the cap. Brooke grabbed it and fell backward in her arms, closing her eyes and holding the bottle herself.

Troy sat the backpack inside the door and leaned against the frame. "I figure you're stressing. Please don't. I can tell you that this was an officially sanctioned operation that turned upside down quicker than anything I've ever worked. Probably because other agencies were involved, and I'm not sure we got the full story. You and Brooke were put in danger and fu—dge me, that scared the crap out of me."

"Good catch. I wasn't the one being shot at." Addy lifted her eyebrow.

"You could have been killed when Bowman rounded the corner."

"So, you knew him?"

Troy nodded. "Recent acquaintance. I spent the night in his company in the middle of the rainforest. As you can tell, it didn't go the way either of us planned."

Addy nodded and tried to piece together what had happened, but there were too many missing pieces. "I'll be okay." She stared down at Brooke, who was still drinking her formula.

"Then I'll shower now." Troy moved away from the door before he turned back. "Just for my own sanity, what happened in the hangar doesn't change anything about how I feel for you. Does it modify how you feel about me?"

Addy chuffed out a soft laugh. "If anything, I think the incident intensified what I feel. The thought of losing you when I just found you scared the shit out of me."

"Language," Troy chided her.

"She's asleep." Addy pulled the bottle from Brooke's slack lips. Then she carefully lifted off the bed and placed Brooke in the crib using the safety harness to secure her into the bed so any turbulence wouldn't jolt her. Whoever owned the aircraft had thought of everything.

"You should take a shower with me." Troy stared at her as if he was starving, but she shook her head.

"No. Sorry, but you really do have an aroma surrounding you. Not sexy."

He frowned. "Is it really that bad?"

"Yes." She nodded. "We'll talk about things that

come up when you don't smell like you've walked through a manure field."

He rolled his eyes. "I can't smell it."

"Then you've lost your sense of smell. Leave, now." She pointed out toward the cabin.

"Just one kiss?"

Addy narrowed her eyes at him. She lifted her hand, pinched her nose closed, and walked over to him. He rolled his eyes and backed into the cabin. "I get it. I'm going." He went into the other bedroom, the larger of the two, and shut the door behind him.

Addy slipped out of the bedroom and shut the door to the galley. She made two huge sandwiches and grabbed a soda taking them to the main cabin. "Here you go."

"Oh, God, I think I'm in love with you. Don't tell Flack." Ice took a huge bite out of one of the sandwiches. "No, I'm totally in love with you. You can tell him." The words came out around the food in Ice's mouth. "Do you need me to watch him?"

The man across from Ice lifted his head, which was no longer under a blanket. "Nah, he's not much of a conversationalist. Seems to think he has constitutional rights against self-incrimination and shit like that."

Addy crossed her arms and glared at the man. "Does the constitution apply in foreign countries?"

Ice slapped the arm of his chair. "See, another reason to love you. Nope. It doesn't, and this guy knows it, too, so he's being a dick just to be a dick."

"Well, there's no way to fix stupid." Addy shrugged. "I'm going to make Flack something to eat. I don't think he's slept, so he'll probably be out for most of the flight."

"Tuck him in for me, will yah? I'm going to stay here with Mr. Delightful."

"I'll do my best." Addy laughed.

"Seriously, if you ever get tired of him, I'll marry you." Ice's yell followed her into the galley. She chuckled to herself and made three sandwiches, then put everything away.

When the bedroom door opened, she laughed. "Those are not your clothes."

"I didn't pull a change of clothes out of my bags, so I borrowed some in the closet." He extended his arms and turned around. Addy covered her mouth and laughed. "The length is a bit long on the slacks, but that shirt." The slacks were made of a deep gray silk and were obviously expensive, but Troy was smaller than the man who owned the suit. The white silk shirt billowed at the waist and poofed over the slacks. Troy chuckled and tucked the shirt in correctly. The waist was cinched with a belt, and the effect wasn't horrible. "I made you something to eat."

"Thank you." He took his plate to the farthest bank of chairs from Ice and the … prisoner? She wasn't sure what was going on there, but one thing was firm in her mind—the man was involved in trying to kill Troy. She cocked her head and looked at him. He glanced up and caught her staring at him. "What?"

"Why were they trying to kill you?" She spoke low so no one else could hear them.

"For something I obtained in the rainforest. I can't tell you any more than that." He took another bite of his sandwich. Addy bit into hers and chewed it as she let the puzzle pieces fall into order. "You didn't expect this to be anything other than a translation job. You said the op went south because other agencies didn't fill you in or left something out. You took something and were chased through the rainforest; however, you escaped and made it back to us to get us out of the country before anyone could take whatever you have away from you."

Flack lifted an eyebrow. "That is totally accurate."

"Except the guy chasing you figured out where you'd go."

"Not the one chasing me. The one he worked with," Flack said in between bites.

"So at least three perps, two are dead, and the one out there believes the Constitution will save his ass, so American." She took another bite and thought for a moment. "They probably stole data of some kind. You didn't return with a package or case. Data would take up much less space. Say a jump drive or CD."

Troy stopped chewing and stared at her. Finally, a sexy-as-hell smirk spread across his face. "You, my dear, will make one hell of a Guardian investigator."

She lifted her soda can to her lips and smirked back at him. "If I were that good, I'd know what kind of data and what agency was giving you shit information."

Flack shook his head. "You do not want that knowledge."

She shrugged. She kind of wanted the information. If another agency weren't playing fair, the heads-up would be a good thing. But she let it go because he'd said it was above her clearance. "Did you get any sleep?"

"No, and no nappuchinos either. Care to take a nap with me?" He took the last bite of his first sandwich.

She leaned toward him and whispered, "I think someone should be awake to help Ice with his charge. Plus, Brooke will be up soon, so I'll take a rain check if you'd offer me one."

"You have an open invitation." Troy leaned across the table, and their lips met.

Addy shivered at the contact, and a wave of sensation rippled over her body. God, the man did it for her. He was everything she'd ever wanted but didn't know she needed. She let the kiss linger for a moment before ending it and moving a fraction of an inch from his lips. She breathed, "The first opportunity we get. I promise." She leaned forward and kissed him again. The same sensation ghosted through her. He was so powerfully male and so magnetic that she had no chance of escaping his field of influence. None whatsoever, and she was more than okay with that terminal sentence.

lack woke about ten minutes before the pilot announced they were cleared for landing. He reached for the small plastic stick holding the SD card and reassured himself once again that the borrowed slacks did not have a hole in the pocket. He'd checked carefully, but still, the idea of somehow losing the card after all that trouble was at the forefront of his mind.

They taxied into a hangar, and although the engine was off and the ground crew worked on chocking the aircraft's wheels, the crew told them the door was not allowed to be opened yet. Flack watched as a garage door rolled up, and four black and no doubt hardened SUVs pulled up beside the airplane. The crew exited the cabin and opened the door, dropping the stairs. "I'll be back to get you," he told Addy and kissed Brooke before heading down the stairs.

Archangel exited one of the vehicles. Flack didn't recognize the young man with him, but he was holding a laptop. "Flack," Archangel said in greeting.

Flack reached into his pocket and extended the stick to his superior. Archangel shifted his weight and leaned his cane against the SUV. He opened the stick and took out the card. With an utter sense of relief, Flack watched as his superior gave the SD card to the man beside him. It was immediately pushed into a slot on his computer. "It isn't locked?" The man gave Archangel a shocked look. After a few taps of the keyboard, he swung the screen toward Archangel. "Is this what you're looking for?"

Archangel nodded. "It is. Can you get any information from where they obtained these files, Ethan?"

"There's always information in the background," the man acknowledged. "And if I can't get to it, I know someone who can show me how to do it."

"Good. I'd like a word in private with Flack if you don't mind." Archangel grabbed his cane which was propped against the door.

"You got it." The man Archangel had called Ethan hopped back into the SUV and shut the heavy door after him.

"The two men killed at the Manaus airport were killed by gang violence. Unfortunate, but when Americans travel, they should pay attention to their surroundings." He stared at Flack.

"Got it, and I agree. We have one who needs to be interrogated. Ice said he's a clam and hasn't opened his mouth."

"I've got just the thing to help him sing like a bird." Archangel turned to his right and lifted his cane. A team of suited men exited the vehicle and headed toward the aircraft. "Now, about your family."

"Sir?"

"I made a few calls. Your guardianship for Brooke has been expedited, and the judge signed off on it. Also, I received a call from the director of Child Protective Services. I take it you and Brooke's social worker didn't mesh?"

"Ah, no, sir. Oil and water, actually. She's a demonic stick figure of a woman. Brooke was terrified of her the second the woman tried to pick her up."

"Ah. I assumed so. As you are now Brooke's legal guardian, there's no need for further home visits. Consider the warp speed processing my present to you for a job well done. Also, your nanny is a hero in the FBI world. I assume she won't want to stay in her current position too long."

"We've talked. When Guardian starts hiring, she'd like an opportunity to interview at Dom Ops as an investigator. Until then, she'll stay with us. She can rehab her knee while she waits. She's sharp, sir. I didn't tell her squat, but with what she saw and the things that happened, she's pretty much figured out the outline of the mission and that it was data that was taken."

Archangel's eyes narrowed. "How's that?"

"She figured out they were coming after me, and as I didn't have a package or case to transport back, whatever I took from them had to be small. Like a disk for data. She's freaking impressive. Dom Ops will have an excellent investigator on their hands."

"Her physical limitations?"

"Her knee will be one hundred percent or close to it by the time an interview rolls around. Her problem is the loss of hearing in one ear, but, sir, that shouldn't influence anything. She was there with Ice backing me up, and she took down Bowman. Triple tap to center mass. No hesitation. She's a professional through and through. She knows how to handle herself."

"Good. Then the last question I have for you is, have you decided what you're going to do?"

Flack nodded and smiled. "Yes, sir, I'll take the research job."

"Perfect. I have a plan for you, and I'm giving you a part-time assistant, but we'll get more into that later."

"Assistant?"

"Someone we trust implicitly. As I said, we'll talk about it later."

The team of men exited the plane, Ice with them. He pointed to the vehicle where the team was placing the detainee. Archangel nodded, and Ice got into the SUV. "I'd like to meet your nanny and thank her for a job well done."

"I'll go get her, sir."

"Oh, Flack?"

"Sir?" He turned to his boss.

"I'd like my suit back when you're finished with it."

Flack couldn't help the smile. "No problem, sir."

He jogged back to the aircraft and up the steps. Addy was sitting with Brooke and glanced up at him when he entered the plane. "Come on. The boss wants to meet you. I told him about you backing up Ice and how you pieced the information together. He's impressed."

Addy stopped picking up Brooke's things. "Impressed or pissed?"

"Definitely impressed." Flack gathered the rest of Brooke's things, and they exited the aircraft. Flack introduced Addy and Brooke to his superior. Archangel once again leaned the cane against the vehicle and opened his hands for Brooke. The girl leaned toward him immediately.

"I have a little girl, too. She's younger than you are." Archangel bounced Brooke and made her smile. He turned back toward Addy. "I have it on the highest recommendation that you'll make an impressive addition to the organization when we start hiring again. I'll ensure the head of Dom Ops has your resume and you're one of the first calls he makes. Although we have serious needs in several categories, so investigator might not be offered to you right away. Regardless, we will find a position to exploit your attention to detail and weapons and tactical knowledge."

"Thank you, sir. But I really don't like sitting in front of a computer." Addy looked at him and shrugged. He got it. She wouldn't do a job she didn't like or wasn't happy in. His respect for her inched up yet again. She was true to herself and wouldn't compromise. Having that exceptional woman in his life and his bed was a blessing from the universe.

Archangel chuckled. "I assure you that the jobs we have opening in the next couple of months are going to be so active that you'll wish for time in a chair." He handed Brooke back to Addy. "You'll be hearing from Dom Ops soon. Flack, the driver and the lead vehicle are at your disposal. Take them home, get out of my suit, then come in for a debrief."

"Roger that, sir." Flack waited until his boss got back in the SUV before escorting Addy and Brooke to the vehicle they'd been given to use. Addy smiled at the car seat installed in the second row of the vehicle. "This organization thinks of everything."

"They're the best there is." Flack got into the front seat after Addy and Brooke were belted in and gave the address to his driver. God, it was going to be good to be home.

CHAPTER 20

*W*ell, it would be good to get home sooner or later. After a quick change and giving Brooke and Addy a kiss, the driver took him back to Guardian, which was where he'd been for the last five hours. He went over every minute of his time in Brazil with Anubis and Fury via video link. "There's one thing that's bothering me. The woman in the village said that Bowman had fed men to the fish." Anubis leaned in. "Was she lying?"

"Who else is missing from the CIA?" Fury asked. "My bet is whoever helped get that list is now at the bottom of the river. But any talk of that now would be speculation since we don't have that information yet. Once we clear the secure comms, we can check for updates. CCS is working on trying to find background information on the card. If there is any system information on it, Jewell will find it. Not that the CIA will admit their fuck ups to any other players."

"They're accountable to someone, aren't they?" Flack stretched his back.

"They have checks and balances, but sometimes even in the best organization, which they're not, shit happens." Fury leaned back in his seat. "All right. We have beaten this dead horse, and it isn't going to get up again. Flack, Archangel said he made you an offer."

"He did, and I'm going to accept it. I can't put Brooke or Addy in danger again." Both Anubis and Fury looked up at the same time. Flack glanced from one to the other. "What?"

"Nothing." A cynical smirk slid across Fury's face. "Not a damn thing. The Rose is clear."

Flack looked at Anubis. "Seriously, what did I say?"

Anubis chuckled. "Nothing we haven't heard before. I'll miss working with you, my friend."

"I'll still be with the organization and probably be out west to visit certain friends. We'll see each other, I'm sure."

"I'll make a point of it. Whatever it takes."

"As long as it takes," Flack said, and the screen went black. He stood up and stretched, popping his back in the process. Smoke was standing in the hall waiting for him when he exited the secure room.

"Got a minute?"

"Yeah, sure. What's up?" Flack wasn't too sure about the look on Smoke's face.

"I don't know how to say this, so I'm going to just put it out there."

"Brooke? Addy?" He tightened, ready to launch out of the facility.

"No, no. Sorry. They're fine." Smoke sighed and ran his hand through his hair. "Brooke's grandma left her house in the middle of the night. Her husband didn't hear her leave. She was only wearing a nightgown and slippers. She must have gotten confused. The police found her three blocks away. It was below zero. She didn't make it."

"Damn it." Flack fell against the wall and held it up for a minute. He'd been upset with Brooke's grandparents until Demos talked him out of it. Damn it. He hated that such a horrible thing had happened to them. He'd reach out to Mr. Shankle and make sure the man saw Brooke as much as possible. Hell, he had that little apartment in the back of the house. Maybe, in time, he'd offer Mr. Shankle a place to stay. It would be hard on the man to be alone after being married for so many years. His mom said loneliness was the hardest thing to get used to after losing a spouse. He shook his head. "I can't imagine what she went through or what her husband is going through now."

"Thought you'd want to know. He's all alone now." Smoke cuffed him on the shoulder. "I'm heading out. You need a ride home?"

"Yeah, thanks. But aren't you in the other direction?"

"I am. Charley is in meetings with other agencies, and I'll be lucky to see her before tomorrow morning. The drive will kill some time."

He followed Smoke through the maze of security and checkpoints. The hotel they'd rented out would never be the same, but then again, Guardian could have purchased it for all he knew. The heavy modifications would have had to be approved if they hadn't.

"It must suck to work different schedules," he commented, thinking about Smoke having time on his hands.

"It isn't often. For the most part, our schedules

are compatible. She makes sure of it." Smoke laughed. "I've never met a bossier, stronger-willed woman." Smoke hit the fob and opened his vehicle.

Flack laughed, "And you love it."

"God, you have no idea." Smoke chuckled as he started the car and put it into Drive.

"Did they get anything out of the guy we brought back?" Flack asked, taking in the ride Smoke was driving. Of course, it was one of the heavy SUVs all the Guardian bigwigs traveled in. Now that Smoke was married to upper management, he rated. Flack wasn't exactly sure where Smoke's wife fell in the hierarchy, but she did something that made her important, which was enough information for him. He was a master at accepting compartmentalized information.

"We got nothing from *him*." Smoke sent him a sideways glance.

Flack caught the meaning. "But?"

"But our computer people found several erased areas in the card. The information that was stolen was placed on the card, and it wrote over the stuff already on it, kind of erasing the areas, but as in all things computer, nothing is ever completely gone."

"They were able to recreate the over-written information?"

"Pictures." Smoke smiled and hit the turn signal.

"Pictures?"

"A birthday party, by the looks of it. Someone decided to use an SD card that they had lying around."

"You've got to be shitting me." Flack felt his mouth drop open and snapped it shut.

"Sadly, I am not. We've found the woman via facial recognition. Guess where she works?" Smoke stopped at a light that had turned red.

"Let me take a wild-assed guess. The CIA. Information processing, maybe?"

"The CIA, foreign operations computer security division."

"Holy shit."

"You got that right. But wait, there's more." Smoke used his best infomercial voice for the last part of that comment.

"What?"

"A group picture at the birthday party. Bowman, Perry, Lucas—that's the man you brought back with you—the woman and two men, both of whom worked at the security checkpoints to the CIA's most classified division." Smoke hooted a laugh.

"Which is how they smuggled the chip out of an area that had to scan people in and out."

"Correct."

"But why Manaus? Why Brazil?"

"Bowman and Perry had both done deep ops in the area, and they had a small hut they'd used during the numerous operations they took part in. It was located about five clicks north and east of where the boat picked you up. He was probably taking you there."

The dark hut that was on the first recording. That made sense now. "So one or both of the security guards decides he doesn't like the play they're making and steals the chip." Flack put the story together.

"Or Bowman and crew were never going to split the money they were planning on getting from selling the list." Smoke added. "My question is, how does Bowman stop them and then toss them into the river, not knowing if they had the disk on them?"

Flack shook his head. "Bowman wasn't brilliant, but he would have made sure he searched the men before he fed them to the fish, which is why he was looking for the card at the place where he stopped them, the Piraha camp, and why they needed a translator. But that doesn't make sense. Perry and his partner were sent down after Bowman."

"They would have been. That was Perry's area of expertise. They were counting on being sent. They had it planned; I can tell you that." Smoke shook his head. "Just think of what that brain power could have done for the good of the world if they'd applied it."

"People like them are too easily tempted by greed."

"Says a person born with a silver spoon in his mouth." Smoke chuckled.

"Granted, but greed doesn't have a banking limit. As you know, most of the people we deal with are rich beyond most people's wildest dreams. They're still corroded by greed and the lust for more power."

"True."

"The CIA has egg on their face." Flack shook his head.

"But the director is standing up and making moves based on this incident. From what I understand, this guy has integrity and isn't interested in politics, so he's fixing shit whether or not it brings attention to the organization."

"About damn time."

"Yeah," Smoke agreed, and they were silent for a long moment. "You made the right call taking Archangel up on the offer, but you'll still be part of this class. Part of the team. We aren't going to let you go."

"Thanks for that." News traveled fast. He wondered when his friends would start popping off texts to him. It was strange that Malice hadn't reached out by now. Maybe he was on an assignment.

FLACK WAVED at Smoke as the man backed out of the driveway. The lights glowed a warm yellow from the windows of the house. He shoved his hands in his pockets and looked at the home. Because that was what it needed to be now. A home.

The front door opened, and Addy stood in the light that spilled from the interior. "Are you going to stand there all night?"

Flack chuckled and made his way up the walk to the front door. He wrapped her in his arms, dropped a kiss on her lips, and backed them into the house, kicking the door shut as soon as they moved past the threshold. "Is she asleep?"

Addy pulled back. "Yes, but …" He chased her lips and grabbed her ass, lifting her so he didn't have to bend over. "No buts. Well, maybe this one." He squeezed Addy's perfectly firm ass.

"Yeah, well, I hope not." Val's voice split the silence. A raucous round of laughter filled the foyer.

Flack's head whipped around to see his entire class. Addy laughed and pulled away. "Your friends are here. Seems they found out about some work-related decision."

Flack dropped his head back. "I'm not going to get lucky anytime soon, am I?"

"Dude, you have the rest of your life for that." Phoenix held up a bottle of amber liquid. Time to celebrate.

Smoke opened the front door and walked in. "It's party time." He rubbed his hands together. "Who brought the food."

"Ice and Malice," Harbinger said from the door of the kitchen. "Reaper sends his congratulations."

"You know, Addy, this will still be our hangout, right?" Malice popped a beer as he spoke.

Flack let her down when she wiggled against

him and responded, "As long as I am here, each of you has an open invitation."

"Hey, what if I'm not okay with that?" Flack looked from person to person.

"Don't be a dick," Aspen said, causing everyone else to laugh.

"I am totally *not* a dick." Flack took a beer from Malice.

"You are," at least four voices said in unison.

Addy put her arm around him and smiled up at him. "Your crew is made up of amazing people."

He smiled and shook his head. "You have no idea."

She tipped her head and winked at him. "I do have an idea. A damn good idea, and I know what you're giving up for Brooke."

"And for you." He dropped to kiss her.

"We'll see." She smiled at him. "Let's not rush things."

"I'm okay with that. As long as I get lucky tonight."

Addy tipped back her head and laughed. "As soon as we have the house to ourselves."

Flack stood up straight. "Okay, everyone. Thanks for coming. Now, get out." He pointed toward the front door.

Several middle fingers flew in his direction, and someone turned on a low stream of music. Harbinger came out of the kitchen with plates. "Food, people." He pointed toward the dining room. Smith offered his arm to Val and led the procession to the dining room.

Addy sighed and tried to hide her smile as she teased, "I don't think they're leaving any time soon."

He lifted his voice so everyone could hear him. "Payback is a bitch." The laughter told them no one cared. All right, if that was how they wanted to play it, he'd find a way to make sure all of them suffered. A smile spread across his lips. Okay, so maybe he was a dick.

FLACK WAVED as the last Uber left the driveway. Then he shut the door and locked it. A quick trip through the first floor making sure lights were turned off and the doors were secured preceded his jog up the staircase toward Addy's room. She'd gone upstairs while he was seeing Malice and Ice out. The assholes had the audacity to suggest a movie marathon. He'd get them back. He smiled as he opened her door. The lights were out. "Addy?" he whispered.

"Over here," she said from his bedroom door. Oh, holy fuck. She wore one of his button-down shirts, and it draped halfway down her thighs.

"Jesus, I'm buying you a thousand of those shirts in every color." The light from his room outlined her tight body under the thin Egyptian cotton.

Pulled to her like a moth to a flame, he once again cupped her ass and lifted her to his lips. That time, there would be no interruptions. He shut the bedroom door and carried her to the bed. The taste of her drove him crazy with need. The night on the plane seemed eons ago, even though it was just days. He lowered her to the bed, and her hands ripped at his shirt. He lifted a bit and helped her shed the material. "No, all of it. Off," she said as her hands fumbled with the fastener of his jeans. "Now," she groaned.

No one needed to tell him twice. He stood up and got naked a second before diving back onto the bed and over the woman driving him insane with need. The kiss started hot and morphed into the nuclear arena. Fuck, she could kiss. Breaking away, he lowered to her breast, feasting on her as her hands traveled his back. Her fingernails raked across his skin when he nipped at her hard, pebbled nipple. Her body arched under him, and he committed her reaction to memory. They were still so new, so fucking good, but new. He wanted to map her body with his mouth, feel every soft curve with his fingertips, and discover the things that drove her insane. He wanted nothing more than to shatter her, only to put her together and make her break again. He kissed his way down her body, using the shirt as his navigational guide. He unbuttoned each of the fasteners and feasted on her skin as he made his way to her core. He spread her legs and fit himself between her thighs. God, the first taste of her was unbelievable. She gasped and grabbed his hair. He held her hips down as he feasted like a starving man. Because he was. He was starving for her in a way he'd never experienced.

She pulled him back up. "I want you to ruin me again." She wrapped her strong arms around his neck, and their tongues dueled as his cock found her core. He entered her with a swift thrust. He consumed Addy's half yell, half gasp, the feeling of her desperation fueling his raging fire. He hilted and withdrew, using fast strokes to slide against all the nerve endings inside her, stopping and grinding against her clit. She undulated under him. He broke the kiss and shifted to his elbows, cupping her shoulders and holding her still under him.

He lost track of time, of place, and of everything except the woman he was with. He was with her in a way he'd never been with another woman. They stared at each other as the tension inside him built. He felt her body tighten and ripple around him. He watched her as she shattered. It was the most beautiful thing he'd ever seen. Troy closed his eyes and followed her over the edge into the abyss of sensation.

Her fingers running through his hair were the first thing that registered. He moved to his side and pulled her into him. "Did I ruin you?" He was finally able to ask the question.

She hummed a sweet sound. "God, yes. I think you ruined me for any other man."

He sighed contentedly and closed his eyes. "I'm more than okay with that."

CHAPTER 21

*S*even Months Later:

"I can't believe Addy took the job at Guardian." Malice sat in the chair in the corner of Flack's bedroom and shook his head. Flack peered back at him through the mirror. "That was never in question."

"But she's supposed to be here with Brooke. Man, you know you're never going to find another nanny like her."

Flack sighed and closed his eyes. "This was her choice, you know it."

"You should have talked her out of it," Ice said

from the doorway. "Smith said he needed to see you before you left."

"Okay. Did you make sure Walter knew what we were doing?" Brooke's grandpa usually stopped by most afternoons. There would be no one at home today. "Yep. Invited him to come to the courthouse, but he said he'd congratulate you tomorrow."

"That's good." Flack looked at himself. The black suit, tie, and shoes were offset by his light purple shirt. "This is okay, right?"

"Absolutely. Don't worry. We'll catch you if you pass out." Malice stood up and grabbed his suit jacket.

"I'm not going to pass out." Flack rolled his eyes.

Ice shrugged, "Okay, fine, we'll let you drop."

Flack shook his head. "Whatever."

"Did you find a new nanny?" Ice asked. "I could be here for the interviews again. I mean, I'd suffer through it again."

"No, I've been through six interviews already. Nobody fits."

"You mean nobody is Addy. You shouldn't have let her leave."

"I didn't let her do anything. She's her own

woman and knows her own mind. It was a mutual decision that I support."

Malice snorted as they walked down the hall to Brooke's room. "Keep telling yourself that, brother."

"Hey, sweetie." Flack ignored his friends and picked Brooke up from the playpen before grabbing the ratty lion she loved. "Ready to go?"

"Go." The little girl had no idea where they were going. "Ice, could you put her in the Escalade while I see what Smith needs?"

"You got it. Come here, princess." Brooke laughed as Ice twirled her around.

Malice grabbed her diaper bag. "We'll meet you outside, and I'll follow you to the courthouse."

"All right. Thanks." Flack adjusted his tie as he hurried down the stairs and to the vault where he and Smith worked together. He keyed the combination to lock, placed his thumb on the pad, and entered. "What's up?"

"The surveillance videos for the hotel's foyer, the elevator, and the hallway to the room have been validated. It was him. He was the only one in that room and the one who exited forty-three minutes later. He was the only one who had the opportunity."

Flack sighed and stared at the screen Smith was pointing toward. "All right, that's damning, but we need to put the man's finger on the trigger. It's one of many elements of the case. The magnitude of the entire package is what will allow us to proceed or force us to admit defeat. Is there any footage from ground level facing toward the building at the time of the incident?"

"I've requested it."

Flack smiled. "I better watch out; you could take my job."

"No." Smith shook his head. "I like the puzzle aspect of what we do here, but the legalities and the nuances of the confirmation or exoneration escape me."

"Well, then, I'll stop worrying. Are you ready?" Flack asked as he headed back to the door.

"I am. I'll close down, lock up, and meet Val at the courthouse. Congratulations, by the way. What a day. Officially becoming Brooke's dad is an awesome thing."

"Man, the adoption was a no-brainer. I'm going to raise that little girl as mine. She'll always know about her real mom and dad, but she deserves a full-time parent, not just a legal guardian."

"You've always done what was right for her. I

suspect you always will. You should go in case there's traffic."

"Yeah, heading out." Flack opened the door and jogged to the SUV. Malice started his car, but Ice was in the back seat with Brooke. He jumped in the driver's seat. "All right, ready or not, courthouse, here we come."

"Will there be food there?" Ice asked as he put the truck into gear, and Flack rolled his eyes. Some things never changed.

"ALL RIGHT, your signature here and here is all that's needed." The judge pointed to the lines where Flack signed his legal name. When Flack put the pen down, the judge smiled. "Congratulations, Dad." The judge extended her hand across her desk, and Flack rose, grasping the woman's offered hand. His crew had been pretty well-behaved until that point. But as soon as he grabbed the judge's hand, confetti flew in the air, and a cheer went up.

He grabbed Brooke from Val and laughed as the little girl tried to catch the streamers that Harbinger popped into the air.

He held up his hand. "Wait, wait, wait." He

waited for the idiot assassins to control themselves. "There's something I want to say."

"As long as you keep it short. I'm hungry," Ice said from the back of the office.

"You're always hungry. But for the sake of your perpetually empty stomach, I'll try. Smith, would you open the door?" The confused looks on the faces of his crew were exactly what he expected. Smith opened the door, then stepped to the side. Addy stood in a white pantsuit at the door. Her father extended his elbow and escorted her into the judge's chamber while her mother followed them through the door and took Brooke from Flack.

"I believe there are two more official acts to complete."

Flack extended his hand. Addy kissed her dad and walked to him. "Judge, we're ready."

"Oh my God! You're getting married!" Val clapped.

Aspen joined in with a cheer, "So wonderful!"

The judge cleared her throat and began the ceremony. Addy smiled up at him and repeated the words. He couldn't have told you what he'd said, but when he slipped that ring on her finger and the judge pronounced them husband and wife, he knew he'd found his heaven with his wife and daughter. He wished his family could have been present, but he hoped they knew in some way that he was happy, in love, and would care for and protect Brooke and Addy with his life.

THE GUARDIAN VETTED caterer set up the reception in Flack's house while they were gone. The white flowers and streamers interspersed with pink balloons turned the sunroom that ran the length of their house into a gorgeous reception hall. Flack had spared no expense on the food or decorations. Addy laughed with not only the Guardians she knew like family but many of her old team who had been invited to the reception. Walter had declined to attend, and she understood. He was a wonderful grandpa to Brooke. He spent many afternoons with her building blocks or walking out in the yard, discovering dandelions.

Flack came up behind her and wrapped his arms around her. "I love you."

She turned in his arms. "I love you, too. Where's Brooke?"

"With Val—no, Aspen." Troy looked over the

heads of most of the people in the room, seeing what she couldn't.

"You know my mom volunteered to watch her on the days you have to work." Addy looked up at her husband. He cocked his head and stared down at her.

"She'd do that?"

"She would. There might be an afternoon or two when Walter would have to fill in, but he said he'd be fine with that." She didn't care for any of the nannies the agency had sent over. Not that they were bad. The women were qualified, but leaving her daughter with them didn't feel right. "I can't believe we adopted her and were married on the same day."

"And kept all these people in the dark."

"I didn't tell Mom until two hours before we were supposed to be at the courthouse. She was so mad. She wanted to get her hair and nails done."

"She looked wonderful but not as beautiful as you." Troy smiled down at her. "But that was a little bit evil, and it was short notice."

"I know, but I also know my mom. After telling them not to tell anyone, she would have told everyone exactly what was going to happen." Addy laughed and leaned into her husband. "Do you remember me signing the adoption paperwork after we signed the marriage certificate?"

"I most certainly do. I wouldn't have missed seeing my wife become my daughter's mother." He started rocking her to the beat of the soft music piped through the sound system. She moved her feet with him, and they began dancing. "When I was in the hospital after the explosion, I never would have dreamed of this. Of you, Brooke, our lives together."

"Sometimes we have to go through hell to find heaven." Troy spun her around and brought her back into his chest. "You are my heaven."

She bowed back so she could look up at him. "And you are my world." He bent down to kiss her, ending that one with several quicker pecks. She sighed and leaned against him again. Addy breathed in the feelings of the moment. The love, joy, and promise of a life filled with laughter, friends, and all the good things in life. She looked up at him. "Today is the beginning, Troy. We are so lucky."

He smiled down at her. "We are. We most definitely are."

*I*ce held Brooke in his arms and danced with her through the crowd of couples. He planned on getting to know several very nice-looking women in attendance. But right now, he was dancing with his niece.

He caught sight of Malice weaving through the crowd toward him and stopped spinning Brooke. He knew that look. He caught Val's eye and handed Brooke to her with a loud kiss on the little girl's cheek.

Malice nodded toward the corner, and Ice made his way to meet his friend. "What's up?"

"Anubis called. You've been tapped."

"Now? Shit." He glanced around the room. "All right. I'll say my congratulations again and then call in."

Malice shook his head. "He said to call in now. I'll make your apologies. We all know the job."

"Yeah, okay. I'm out."

"Ice?"

"Yeah?"

"Be careful." Malice pointed at him. "Don't get yourself killed. I'd have to follow you to hell and kick your ass."

"I'd say the same thing." He winked at his friend and headed out of the celebration. As he walked out of the house, he shed the lingering joy, the sense of merriment, and the pretense that he was a normal part of society.

He wondered what kind of bastard he'd be hunting. Not that it mattered. He smiled a wicked grin. He fucking loved the hunt. His mentor had named him Ice for a reason. He was an ice-cold killer, and he was the one they sent in when an operation had the opportunity to get messy. He inspected his car and got in. It was time to become the bringer of death once again. He'd defend those who could not defend themselves because he was not only a Guardian—he was a Shadow.

He dialed the phone and put his car into gear. The voice on the other end put things in perfect order. "Operator Two Seven Four. Good evening, Sunset Operative Sixteen. Standby for transfer to the Annex."

Ice felt the power of those words flow through him. Guardian had been dealt a blow, but his organization had survived. Guardian Security, in all of its power and glory, was back.

Novella

Montana Guardian: A Kings of Guardian Novella

Guardian Defenders Series

Gabriel

Maliki

John

Jeremiah

Frank

Creed

Sage

Bear

Guardian Security Shadow World

Anubis (Guardian Shadow World Book 1)

Asp (Guardian Shadow World Book 2)

Lycos (Guardian Shadow World Book 3)

Thanatos (Guardian Shadow World Book 4)

Tempest (Guardian Shadow World Book 5)

Smoke (Guardian Shadow World Book 6)

Reaper (Guardian Shadow World Book 7)

Phoenix (Guardian Shadow World Book 8)

Valkyrie (Guardian Shadow World Book 9)

Flack (Guardian Shadow World Book 10)

Ice (Guardian Shadow World Book 11)

Hollister (A Guardian Crossover Series)

Andrew (Hollister-Book 1)

Zeke (Hollister-Book 2)

Declan (Hollister- Book 3)

Hope City

Hope City - Brock

HOPE CITY - Brody- Book 3

Hope City - Ryker - Book 5

Hope City - Killian - Book 8

Hope City - Blayze - Book 10

The Long Road Home

Season One:

My Heart's Home

Season Two:

Searching for Home (A Hollister-Guardian Crossover Novel)

Season Three:

A Home for Love

STAND ALONE NOVELS

A Heart's Desire - Stand Alone

ABOUT THE AUTHOR

Wall Street Journal and USA Today Bestselling Author, Kris Michaels is the alter ego of a happily married wife and mother. She writes romance, usually with characters from military and law enforcement backgrounds.

Made in the USA
Coppell, TX
24 April 2023

15977832R00162